The Secret Voice

The Secret Voice

S T O R I E S

by Gaetan Brulotte

TRANSLATED BY MATT COHEN

The Porcupine's Quill, Incorporated

CANADIAN CATALOGUING IN PUBLICATION DATA

Brulotte, Gaétan, 1945-
[Surveillant. English]
The secret voice

Translation of: Le surveillant.
ISBN 0-88984-097-0

I. Title. II. Title: Le surveillant. English.

PS8553.R825S9713 1990 C843'.54 C90-093771-8
PQ3919.2.B783S9713 1990

Published by The Porcupine's Quill, Inc., 68 Main Street, Erin, Ontario NOB 1TO with financial assistance from the Canada Council and the Ontario Arts Council. Originally published in French by Les Quinze, 1982, as *Le Surveillant.*

Distributed by The University of Toronto Press, 5201 Dufferin Street, Downsview, Ontario M3H 5T8.

Edited for the press by Doris Cowan. Cover is after a photograph by Tony Urquhart entitled *Le Tréport.*

Printed and bound by The Porcupine's Quill.
The stock is Zephyr laid, and the type, Ehrhardt.

Table of Contents

The Sentry

YOU HAVE TO watch the wall. Constantly be on your guard. You can't make a mistake. Always maintain the same distance between the foundations and your feet. Absolutely no leaning against the stone surface. Or putting your hands in your pockets. You remain on the spot; no walking, no speaking, no smoking, no laughing, rifle in hand, ready for anything.

Those are my orders. And they are to be followed to the letter. That is another order. To be followed to the letter. And that is another.... Good, that will do.

My first day on the job, I had to find a place in front of the wall, I mean a good place. How to solve that problem? The ruins of the old structure are about twenty metres long. Of course I could have put myself anywhere, so long as I was close enough to touch the wall when I needed to.

But to practise an efficient surveillance, one both protective and protected, a strategic location was called for. I thought it over carefully and then, having taken account on the one hand of the length, the height, the thickness of this pile of masonry, and on the other hand of the direction of the wind, its estimated velocity, as well as the angle of the sun, I found it right away. Don't ask exactly how I did it. By the end of the day, with a stroke of my heel, I had marked my place: it was the only one possible. Just like that I took up my position next to the wall. Moreover, the former commandant complimented me on my judicious choice.

That's the way I operate now. I always begin by defining my field of activity. That, I think, is the proper method. I used to work quite differently. I tried to do too much at once. I wanted to follow every road blindly, burn everything, laugh. You want to know how to go crazy and die? I have the secret, believe me. My key? Spread yourself thin. The answer to everything? Fire. Destroy and sneer: something always comes of that. At the very least, the pleasure of causing trouble. 'There's your weakness,' my former boss said to me one day. 'You want to be everywhere but you're nowhere. In the future control your breathing.'

I don't know if I really understood him, but I changed my method. I began to regulate my breathing. Thanks to this new technique I am less jumpy and I work more effectively. In fact, I used it to mark off my war zone around the wall.

Did I choose the best site? I think so. In any case the chief, the old one, while inspecting the first evening, said nothing. Which is as good as being commended. And today – still – after all these years of standing guard, I don't regret my choice. But neither am I proud of it. I may seem indifferent but the truth is I am only trying to be objective.

***

Recently a new commandant was named – more rigid, more intransigent than the first. According to the authorities the previous one, through time and bad habits, had gotten soft – obviously unacceptable given our situation. But even my present superior has found nothing to reproach me with when it comes to my position with regard to the wall.

***

Sometimes I wonder why I have spent my whole life here. No doubt it was my fate. I don't know exactly what that means, but it provides a little consolation. Why haven't I left this job? Why do I not, even today, hand in my resignation? I can't. I would be sorry to leave the wall. It's part of my life now: this decrepit fallen-down rockface is – in its way – me. If I abandon it a piece of my own soul might collapse. Of course I'd gladly leave it if I could take it all with me. But have you ever heard of anyone who could take his place with him? No, that really wouldn't work. Anyway, I suppose I must be satisfied with this job since I haven't quit. And when you think you've found a real sinecure, I don't see why you wouldn't keep it. And I like my wall. I've spent so much time with it, I've gotten to know it. During the day, soaked in warmth, in the hard dazzling light, it seems to be happy that I'm here. It accepts me, which is something.

I would even say that behind its impassive appearance it is driven by secret needs. It wants to communicate. Sometimes it really seems to want to touch me. Then it stretches out like an arm. Or hardens like a sexual organ. It calls me. Who knows what it wants. Anyway, under the midday sun, I sense in it a whole world simmering with tension and rage. The time will come when I'll say to it, 'Speak to me.' And it will.

At night it's easier for us to be close. I move against it. I love to bathe in its cave-like smells and to feel, through its cold skin, a cosy heat rising. It lives: it gives off a certain breath and, towards evening, it softens. Its fibres relax. It sleeps. For a long time I watch over it. Because here, even asleep, your mind is alert. Doesn't danger prefer to arrive in the dark? So I sleep a bit less at night and doze a bit more during the day, standing up, without appearing to do so. A simple matter of common sense.

For the contemplation of my wall, I have all the time in the world. I do not have the right to look away. The new boss thinks everything depends on this bit of fallen-down rampart. So it's obvious that everything depends on me. Who guards the wall? Who is always here? Who wards off the menace? Who is always ready to confront the enemy? Who is ready for whatever might happen? Who is always on the alert so that no incident can arise? Who if not I? Take away the guard and the wall serves no purpose. Oh, I know, my current boss has the answer to that argument: 'Take away the wall,' he says, 'and the guard becomes unnecessary.' An elementary logical trap in which he hopes to catch me. You mustn't let yourself be dragged into that. That's why I never argue with him. I have my own opinions and I keep them to myself. Or I confide them to the wall, you can trust it, it knows how to keep quiet – and silence is the path of wisdom.

The chief of the moment, for his part, isn't fond of silence. He suspects that my terseness is hypocrisy. He detests mystery. He has always lived, so he says, in the bright light of reason. He checks the guard eight times a day. He criticizes me for all sorts of trifles: for example, singing on the job (against regulations) or forgetting to bury my garbage (that's the rule). What can you do? When you are working, you can't think of everything. Once he caught me laughing at some private joke. I must have been daydreaming. But I was deviating from the rules. I wasn't taking my job seriously. He gave me a reprimand and threatened to dismiss me. 'First and last warning,' he stated categorically.

* * *

Since that little slip on my part the commandant has redoubled his inspections. With his binoculars he spies on me from his sentry box. He has even posted a number of colleagues in various places to inform on my behaviour and file reports. Doubtless he believes that I haven't noticed, but I'm not the fool he thinks I am.

Moreover, from time to time he shows up unexpectedly to see if I am fulfilling my duty to perfection, and to test me. One evening, at the ambiguous hour of twilight, and he chose that time on purpose, he arrived from headquarters accompanied by a man in plain clothes. I spotted them both right away, despite the difficulty and distortion of vision at that transitional moment of the day. 'Who goes there?' I said instantly, following regulations. 'It's me, Pim, your brother,' the disguised person replied. 'Who goes there?' I repeated. 'It's me, your brother,' the other insisted. 'I've come to visit you.' Of course I recognized the game. The boss had instructed him not to give the password; or, indeed, had not even told him of its existence and importance. Just that, out of spite, and just to see what would happen – to test me. I cocked the hammer of my rifle, loudly, so that the fake brother would understand, and then I raised it, finger on the trigger. 'Identify yourself!' I shouted at him, by way of ultimatum, 'or I shoot!' There was a long silence. In the restricted field of vision of my sights the man continued to advance. I wanted to tell him to turn back. For a moment I even thought he might be joking. But the boss, a bit to the side, was watching the scene. The stranger who accompanied him spoke again. 'It's me, Pim, your brother. I'm bringing you some food and a present from the family.' I almost softened. Sometimes you get careless and catch yourself thinking. You have to avoid that. But nothing prevents you from preserving a certain dignity. You just have to close your eyes to a few little details. And do the job conscientiously. Anyway, I can't think while I'm working. The problem takes care of itself. I do not have the right to allow my wall to be threatened. I do not have the right to believe all this sand is foreign to me and not a part of myself. That evening I heard the light footsteps of the person who was pretending to be my brother. I more or less made out his body in the blurred twilight. I felt the blood pulsing in my temples, felt my shoulders slacken, my legs flex, my whole body grow weak. This is absurd, I told myself. I was trembling. But suddenly I could see the black stain of the commandant at the far edge of my vision. At once my body righted itself. My breathing deepened, my back stiffened, my eyes hardened and my finger tightened on the trigger. A dry whistling sound had just shaken the sombre tranquillity of the wall and the innocence of the setting sun. The shot came so fast that I heard it only in my imagination – and without really believing it. The silhouette of the civilian twisted and collapsed with a clatter of mess-tins. I realized that I had just accomplished an heroic deed. Nothing special, boss. Everything is in order, boss. That night I had no dinner.

***

Another day there was someone behind the rampart – perhaps it was another of my new superior's tricks. Silent enemies must have been hiding on the other side of the wall, since a stone fell quite close by, as if someone had wanted to hit me. The projectile buried itself idiotically in the sand, two steps away, with all the force of its weight. Of course I guessed the trap. They weren't going to trick me. They were just trying to distract me. It was obvious. Just the same, someone with my experience is not so easily duped. That trivial little object didn't worry me for long. I was startled, but I barely turned my head – just a split-second reflex. Of course I didn't pick it up. That must have been their strategy: to divert my whole attention to it. The classic ambush, in a word. But I wasn't fooled. I stayed where I was. Why move? – I had long ago settled on the best place to stand. And my reaction must surely have confused them. In that totally unexpected way I kept control of the situation. They realized immediately who they were dealing with. Boss's trick or enemy probe? It made no difference to me; whoever it was gauged my strength and decided not to try again. Because there were no more falling stones.

That is how I am in my work: uncompromising. It's the only way to succeed. And the fact that I get such good results speaks for itself. A question of common sense.

***

What use is this wall? you might ask me. Rampart? Fence? Windbreak? Is its function to protect, to defend, to stop, to slow, to hide, to contain, to restrict, to divert? Or is it simply a matter of deception? Something to keep men busy? Many others have asked themselves these questions. As demonstrates this quasi-response, if you need one, written on a section of the wall by my predecessor, more than twenty-five years ago. 'I am useless.' But who is this 'I': the wall or the guard? There are some people, as is well known, who need to feel useful at any cost. Perhaps my predecessor was one of those. Be that as it may, these questions are beside the point. The wall exists. It must be watched. If only to commemorate the courage of those sentinels who spent their lives beside it. Might it therefore serve as a monument? If nothing else, might this crumbling parapet not be seen as a kind of enormous honour roll? Might this decayed mound of rocks have, in the end, no meaning? Impossible. The boss says there is always a meaning. A wall is necessary and the walls justifies the means.

This knowledge has given me the strength to hold out for more than a quarter century. I'm like that. A nothing can encourage me. A trinket converts me. A trifle changes the whole course of my life. Which is what happened to me when I began to write this text. I didn't like the soup one evening, and I just let myself go.

***

There it is. My cards are on the table. I've won or lost, who can say, it all depends on your point of view. In fact the boss just caught me red-handed. I didn't hear him coming. Did he crawl silently along the wall? I wouldn't put it past him. It happened today at noon, a totally unexpected moment when – for the second time in my whole career – I was not guarding the wall. I didn't realize what I was doing. Had I slid, unaware, from vigilance to dreaming? Sometimes you pass from one state to the other without realizing or knowing why. But when you have a job like mine, such a slip is clearly unforgivable. I want to insist on the fact that I am not being lenient with myself. My superior caught me at fault in my work: in such circumstances I am in the wrong and he is justified in his harshness. My case will serve as an example to my colleagues.

Here I reconstruct, as well as I can, the brief altercation we had, the commandant and I, at that unhappy moment when I was day-dreaming, my head bent over my writing-pad, and my pen – instead of my rifle – in my hand.

'What are you doing?' he suddenly asked me in a peremptory tone.

I started violently and, straightening up, responded without hesitation: 'Nothing to report, boss.'

'And that?' he pursued, pointing his finger at the notebook and pen which I was trying vainly to hide.

As I hesitated, wondering whether I should tell him the truth, he ordered me to explain, immediately, these unusual objects as well as my bizarre activities.

'It's okay, boss,' I said, opting for the naïve approach, 'I was just taking notes.'

In fact I was writing the above text. I wanted to set it down on paper. I don't really understand why.

'And the wall?' he retorted angrily.

He was in the right. But who isn't? I put my writing things in my pocket so that I could get back to work. I didn't really think I would get off so easily. But I didn't foresee the enormous repercussions of my error. Nor did I realize that the boss was so excessively punctilious. Certainly I expected some consequences, but not the radical punishment to which I was subjected.

'And what have you been writing?' he persisted.

'I've started my memoirs,' I confessed.

'Your memoirs!' he cried out. He was astonished but there was also an unmistakable note of contempt in his voice.

'Yes, my memoirs,' said I, with a mixture of pride and fear because I could not predict his reactions.

'And how far have you got?' he continued mockingly.

'To the wall,' I told him.

'To the wall, *sir*,' he insisted with a touch of insolence.

'To the wall, sir,' I repeated.

A long silence followed. He spread his legs, crossed his arms, stared at me. I didn't know where to look. I swivelled my eyes to the top of the wall. I caught myself hoping an enemy would appear to put an end to this embarrassing situation.

'Why not a novel about the wall, while you're at it?' he said, smiling as though he found my initiative deeply irritating. His flinty tone required no reply.

'Of course you know,' he went on in his calm and authoritative voice, 'that you have absolutely no right to indulge yourself in this way during working hours or to allow your surveillance of this area to lapse. One moment of inattention and everything could be lost. You occupy a post which demands of its holder an exact sense of responsibility. The lives of several people are in your hands. You must be reliable. You know it well. At the beginning you seemed to be an exemplary employee. The wall, under your guard, stood. It had, as they say, a certain panache. You gave it that indefinable extra. We used to be proud of you. Moreover, your dossier was clean. It must be said, however, that my predecessor did not always demonstrate the necessary attention to duty. Doubtless you've been used to things being easier, more relaxed. Nevertheless I warned you the last time I caught you daydreaming on the job. The task of guarding this old structure is not meant for dreamers. Success here requires exceptional abilities. This is a strategic place. Your negligence could lead others to believe that this bit of wall lost in this deserted region has no meaning. In this work, nothing is more dangerous than a casual attitude. Thus for fundamental reasons of security, and also to ensure that your error will serve as an example to others as I am sure you understand, you find us obliged to relieve you of your duties. We know you will weep over the loss of your job. You will miss the wall and the honour attached to its surveillance, you will tell us. Every man here envies your post. We do not lack well-trained and disciplined replacements. Probably you know all this.'

For several minutes he continued along this line. Then he was silent again, for a long moment. Finally, to conclude with the guillotine, he added: 'Your dismissal will take effect tomorrow at dawn.'

Then he left.

What good would it have done to reply? For the moment it was enough just to control my breathing: because this still might have been a trick by the boss to see if I could keep calm in an extreme situation. I could have thrown myself at his feet, pleading with him to forgive me, to let me make amends, to give me a last chance to regain his confidence and that of the group. I chose to show restraint. He turned his back on me decisively, without even saluting, without, moreover, saying goodbye. My memoirs had just stopped short.

***

I spent some time convincing myself that I had really been dismissed. But, with much renunciation, I accepted the idea, as I had to, quite quickly. I spent my last night by the wall trying to re-experience all the great moments I had known in its company and, in particular, the most recent: my heroism in the episode of my so-called brother, my victory over the stone, and finally this last defeat – to be blamed, everything taken into account, on writing. I put a little time into engraving this inscription on the wall – to relieve myself of guilt, as though I were writing my own epitaph: 'I am against those who write on walls.' I'd like to copy it a hundred times, like a grade school punishment.

So here I am a bit before dawn, thinking about the scorpion: in a desperate situation he prefers suicide to surrender. I understand that I could indeed draw the sand over me, hide myself in it and stay here forever, and no one would ever think of looking for me here. I have a right to all this warm sand. Because, in the end, whose is it, and who is it? They will think that I have left, and will leave me in peace with my wall, with myself. Just like that. There you are. It's so simple. It will be completely dark. I don't ask anything more. Just to be myself in the night, where there are no more words. Where the eyes cannot see. The body no longer receives blows from outside, the bombardment of lights. It becomes immune to attack. It retreats into its shell, squeezes shut its orifices, turns off its fountains, its sweat, its urine, its saliva, its words. Just like that. There you are. Peace. No more boss, no more desire. It's so simple. I've got it at last. You always get it sooner or later. And someone will perhaps find, pressed against the foundation, as though they were part of it, my guilty pages blackened with ink.

The Sweeper

WE'RE OFF. The motorcycle flies away, its chrome dazzling the street, dizzy with speed; it almost soars, as though liberated from gravity's cage, throwing its euphoric challenge to the low and ponderous sky.

The offices have just closed, but the stores are still open. The passersby seem hurried on this late autumn afternoon. The weather is gloomy. The clouds rumble. The wind flaps on its hinges. Leaves flutter their panic and are scattered. The world fills suddenly with meaning.

Red light. Stop. At the line, the idling motorcycle grows impatient. It vibrates and growls jerkily. As if to curse the dense city traffic.

Green. Let's go. Gas pours into the cylinders. Mutterings become a series of explosions. Their noise quickly reaches a peak. The street, lit by its walls of store windows and pulsing to the flash of neon signs, rhythmically inhales a new mass of cars. In and out of this slow-moving herd, the motorcycle dodges – agile, weightless, ethereal. A powerful untamed Pegasus, it prances in the midst of the roadway, refusing to fall into step. With each excess it grows wilder, more triumphant. It ignores both the traffic signs of the city and the indicators on its own dials. The faster it plunges ahead, the more sparks shower out of its flaming exhaust pipe, the more it seems to be becoming flight itself.

Each time he accelerates the pilot breaks more of the bonds holding him to earth, forgets the boring flatness of things and their prison of gravity to taste the joy of ascent. His body is wedded to the machine: a feeling of power lifts him, the noise gives him wings; the ego and the engine fuse to become a single impressive display of pure force. The last earthly limits begin to yield and, hair whipping like a flag, the rider feels that the universe is at his fingertips, his fiefdom. By manipulating a throttle, a clutch and a gearshift, he is suddenly akin to the ancient mythological gods who, with a simple gesture, release thunder and wind. From the height of this dominion he weighs also, in his absent-minded way, all the fragility of human creation: his eye, drunk with speed, immediately forgets everything it has succeeded in glimpsing. To him the urban landscape seems a cloth-and-cardboard set put up for one dizzying moment, that of his amnesiac passage. Theatrical façades ready to be taken down fly by on each side and slip into the ephemeral past of the rearview mirror before finally being swallowed by sharp gulps at each new throatful of cool air.

Ah! The exquisite pleasure of speed. To go ever faster, to explore the capacities of a force as elemental as that of an engine. The temptation to accelerate is irresistible, because by constantly living in danger, the pilot gets used to narrowing his margins and with a casual eye measures the gradual shrinking of the gap. Now the motorcycle is running at full speed. It passes a last row of cars to arrive like a whirlwind at a crossing beyond which – finally – there seems to be a path unobstructed.

Suddenly the long peal of a horn pierces the muffled, industrious rumbling of the street. Brakes screech. The grand pandemonium of collision. The crash of broken glass. Everything happens in a quick jumble.

Then everything stops. There is no more movement.

Here and there a few colourless beings are fixed to the spot, as though stitched – so many dolls – in their moleskin bags, and watch – frozen – the spectacle. An accident happens so quickly. It is not easy to understand how these things happen. It's always like that.

There is no movement.

Icarus has lost his wings. Skidding, swerving, the metal horse, in wanting to avoid a pedestrian, leapt sideways, caromed into a car, and rebounded with a flash of chrome into a lamp post. As for the hero of the skies, he has been thrown far away: he lies squashed on the cobblestones, in the gutter, near a sewer, the lower part of his body completely broken. Reality abruptly takes up its cruel solidity and re-establishes its kingdom.

Nevertheless, the bloodied and dishevelled head of the motorcyclist still stirs. But slowly. Little by little, everything becomes as before. The passersby continue their window shopping and don't even notice what is at their feet. Traffic resumes its rhythm, once more at the crossroads there is that steady alternation of braking and acceleration. The cars manoeuvre more skilfully to avoid the body of the hurt man but, despite all their precautions, some cars inevitably drive over what remains of his legs. As for the ruined motorcycle – it was quickly pushed to the side of the roadway. People do what they can. They really behave very well. Just the same, you can't ask too much of them. This is the time when offices are closing. People want to finish their shopping and get home. That's entirely normal. There's enough work to be done during the day. People have neither the time nor the desire to get involved in somebody else's troubles.

The dying man raises his eyes and – in a final effort – dragging himself through his own blood, tries to pull himself onto the sidewalk because, he has realized, he is blocking traffic. Say what you like, social conscience still survives, even at the heart of the most extreme inner panic.

The vague odour of gasoline released to the street by the fall of the motorcycle doesn't seem to trouble the passersby. That, at least, is some consolation. But suddenly the situation takes a turn for the worse. The sky, overcast all day, gradually opens up and then – as though it had all this time been waiting for the signal – releases a torrential downpour. The drops fall by the thousand, by the million. Mixed with hard white hailstones. The forecast predicted this. Cold rain mixed with hail. The pedestrians, faces pinched, are especially taken by surprise. But the rain makes the merchants happy, because shoppers run for the shelter of the stores. Windshield wipers are turned on. Engines lose patience with the stop light.

The dying man pushes his face into the pavement and tries

once again to lever his encumbering body out of the public roadway. But his efforts are in vain. He is unable to move. His hindquarters are stuck to the ground like skin on frozen metal. Exhausted, he still lifts his head and opens his mouth to call or to regain his breath.

Green light. Time to go. The throbbing of the traffic begins again. There is furious honking at that thing in the street. It seems to be a drunk. People curse him, shout at him to get out of the way. His voice wants to reply, but makes no sound.

***

Because of that stare fixed on me, there is a sudden change in atmosphere: a sudden warmth seems to rise up all around. This broken lump of meat is staring at me, but with a strangely melting plea. I admit that this gaze, in distress, and for that reason forceful, intimidates me – suffering, despite what you hear, is a kind of power. And as it doesn't leave me for an instant, it forces me to act. I lower my eyes and I keep sweeping. I do my work as best I can. The boss seldom has reason to reproach me about that. Briefly I yield to weakness once more, and from under my eyelid I look at the dying man. His eyes hover on the edge of consciousness, implore. But what can I do? He is keeping me from my work. What if the boss were to come by? I can already imagine his anger. 'Sweep away that mess. That's an order. What are you waiting for? You want me to report you?'

Before, when I was just learning the job, it would have been possible for me to make a mistake. I would have been forgiven on the grounds of inexperience. Before, I could have gone to one side, I could have pretended not to see him. But now it's not possible to ignore him.

'Sweep away that mess! That's an order!' I know my job now. My boss relies on me. So everything must be cleaned. And when you're a professional, as I am, nothing could be simpler. First, take off the manhole cover. Then, holding the broom firmly as if you were scraping up a giant wad of gum, brace the handle under your armpit to make a solid lever – if necessary, pushing with a foot as well – and, shove the thing into the hole. Like that. After that, a few swipes with the broom on the remains with a bit of water. And then it's all gone. Everything is a question of technique. Before, I probably could not have pulled it off. Now, I have attained a certain perfection in my work. That I know, though I might know nothing else. I have my certificate. In a trade, nothing can equal experience: it's something that can't be bought. Ask the boss.

Discussion Group #96 on General Points

AS IS THE CUSTOM M. Rossi chairs the meeting and Mme Berg volunteers to record the deliberations. Someone questions, on the grounds of the principle of equality, the fact of a woman acting as secretary. M. Stack is therefore suggested. He accepts provided that leniency is granted him due to his inexperience – an indulgence that is willingly and immediately accorded.

***

The president makes an efficient beginning to the evening by quickly reading the brief report of the Commission to Study General Objectives. He moves it be adopted as read. This proposal receives unanimous assent. Following a rapid reading, we also deal with the minutes of the last meeting.

The president announces that a new discussion will be opened on the subject of our earlier undertakings and in order to more precisely survey the opinions of the members present on the objectives to be pursued by our association.

It is now the turn of the assembly to speak. Each person may express his point of view, says the president, provided that he doesn't take too long (he places his watch on the table), provided that he does not stray from the topic, provided that he raises his hand and has his name taken down before speaking, provided that he speaks in order and without interrupting, provided that ... (a few elements of procedure are missing).

The meeting is opened to the floor.

A long silence begins.

At the insistence of the president, Mme Kegg provides the inaugural effort with great simplicity, in bringing the group's attention to a error in the last official Hansard of the society, page 5079, sixth line of the first paragraph. It should read 'Association for Ileitis and Colitis' rather than 'Association for Elitists and....' Mme Lucie Wyck raises the problem of repetitiveness during our meetings. She recommends eliminating anything that might create this impression of repetition.

M. Tarb replies that the repetition of which Mme Lucie speaks is in fact only apparent. The numerous meetings of the Special Objectives Committee to Establish the General Direction, over which he presided, have convincingly demonstrated that repetition does not appear as one of our constants.

Mme Wyck requests that the assembly, while addressing itself to the president, refrain from calling her Mme Lucie. She has already explained herself on this subject several times. This form of address is suited to the proprietresses of brothels and seems disrespectful to her.

In response to movements in the room against this susceptibility judged excessive, the president calls for order and asks that the desire of Mme Wyck be respected.

M. Poquey speaks vigorously against the possible elimination of coffee and cakes at the meetings. He insists on the necessity of maintaining a tradition of minimal services to assure the full effectiveness of our meetings. The presence of the members, their degree of attention to the problems, the willingness of our circle to act may depend, according to him, on such details, which are essential to the quality of life.

The president puts aside the order of speakers already noted to ask Mme Cobb, the hostess of the evening, to immediately enlighten M. Poquey with regard to this subject. Mme Cobb says that there has never been any question, to her knowledge, of eliminating the refreshments.

M. Poquey replies that he thought he had heard something in the corridor before the meeting. He declares himself reassured by the statements of Mme Cobb and invites her, therefore to carry out her duties.

Mme Finn, invoking equality once more, declares herself opposed to the fact that a woman is playing the role of hostess.

Mme Cobb protests that, nevertheless, she enjoys it. But M. Poquey is proposed. While he serves the coffee, the debate continues.

M. Janet thinks, as founder of the association, that this evening may be the turning-point of our history: our collective existence seems increasingly threatened, and if we don't take things as seriously as we ought, we are going to have to dissolve the corporation. He threatens to read the assembly the numerous papers he has brought, which spill over onto neighbouring tables. But there are so many disapproving looks he decides against it. He only carries out a quick survey of the thoughts raised by the Committee for the Study of General Objectives. These remarks bring up again the necessity for an effort to define the direction of our own group. Several trial approaches have been made to various participants in our numerous committees on specific objectives, but at the very most they point to a possibility of sketching out an outline of the subject. The present assembly remains the appropriate place to set in motion any movement for overall agreement.

M. Thub raises the question of whether we should draw up a list of the totality of initiatives tried up to now in the various committees where definition of structure has become an issue. Should we not assemble all the elements necessary to define our objectives, both general and specific? He advances the opinion that the initial aim in the short term, indeed immediately, might in fact be to list all the particulars in terms of time and space, and – for that task – to seek the support of the authorities and major social institutions. This initiative would have the merit of creating a possible alternative and putting us on the road to a conclusive solution. With the means gathered and available for a possible concerted action, we could doubtless amplify the impact of our initiative towards the establishment of general objectives.

M. Tarb reminds us that the desire for external support cannot be given as a general objective.

Everyone hears M. Tromb, who is eating slices of dried bananas from a large transparent bag. As all turn to face him, he blushes all over and offers some to his neighbours. Mme Finn complains about the work of M. Poquey. She hasn't had any coffee. M. Poquey says he is trying to serve people in the order of the seating arrangement.

The president rejoins the battle to set out the two points of view between which we must choose. Our society must tend to be either more open or more closed. The association is at a crucial point in its history: never has it been confronted with such a dilemma. And today we have the possibility of calmly looking at it together, reflecting on the situation, seeing the extent of its scope and finding a solution. We have a problem, he says, perhaps even problems. But all together we should be able, with a common accord, to decide along which path of the future we shall travel.

To finish he scratches some statistics onto the blackboard behind him. These figures show that our membership shrinks from year to year. Now we are only sixty-nine.

M. Seil, laughing, makes a joke concerning the rather erotic character of this number.

M. Brodsky, not laughing, offers a scholarly decoding: six is the number symbolic of ordeals, and nine expresses the end of a cycle, the completion of a journey, the closing of the circle. This figure, according to him, is extremely ominous.

M. Renoti, finger raised, warns the assembly not to overvalue the membership and its quantity. It means less than one would think.

Mme Cobb proposes, at her wit's end, she says, because she feels so far away at the back of the room, the creation of a commission to study ways of defending the interests of our guild (her word) and to examine possible ways of promoting ourselves to the general public. This commission would, specifically, have the task of establishing systems of recruitment and sample advertisements. She would like to take an active part in this.

The president reminds us that our task is to determine our general objectives. The discussion is to bear precisely on this point and no other. He has given us the figures only in order that we may take account of the changing situation in the expression of our points of view.

Mme Vender thinks, unlike M. Renoti, that it is absolutely essential to keep a close eye on the size of our membership.

Mme Grave is anxious that the former objectives, that is to say the current objectives, be maintained. She put them forward, she states, some time ago – before going on maternity leave – and now she would like to have the opportunity to test what their effects would be if they were seriously tried.

The president leads the discussion back to the general objectives to be given to our society. Mme Grave was speaking about very partial and specific objectives which are being totally revised.

Mme Kegg invokes the no-smoking rule which has already been voted on, page 256 of our minutes, and which is to be found in article 5, dash 1, point 2 of our internal rules of order.

In accordance with her wishes, the president asks the smokers to either butt out or bow out.

M. Thub, pounding his fist on the table, declares we are not a deliberative assembly but a consultative one, and that we have no powers – those having been voted to the executive council of the company (his word).

The president contests that and affirms that we do have powers. He throws the debate back to the members.

M. Tarb resumes. He emphasizes that the extent of the membership constitutes only one element of the re-evaluation of our general objectives and that its importance must not be exaggerated.

M. Tytell puts forward the following arguments: many meetings have already been held on the objectives of our club [*sic*]; attendance has varied from one meeting to the next; the definition of our role has not significantly developed since this date last year. He would like to propose that the round of meetings be concluded and that, provisionally, the question be left in abeyance.

The president says he can understand this impatience. Nevertheless, so long as our objectives are not clearly redefined, it will be impossible to act.

M. Tytell replies that we have consecrated all our energy to that since our founding, but that we have actually done nothing.

The president responds by praising the sense of planning our community has shown. We should be happy to realize that we refuse to act blindly. As for the discussion groups, he adds, they take place with the frequency laid out by our statutes and regulations.

M. Tytell affirms that we are wasting our time by meeting so often, and without a precise goal, that this shows a great incapacity to be decisive, that the relevant statutes must be changed in order to reduce the number of meetings. This measure would have the effect, according to him, of reducing the alarming rate of absenteeism and of making our assemblies more effective. He points out that the present meeting, with twenty-three members out of sixty-nine in attendance, does not constitute a quorum and is therefore not democratic.

The president intervenes again to say that the idea of setting a quorum was rejected by vote at a previous meeting because its overly strict application would render inoperative the compulsory meetings of our association. If M. Tytell would like that decision reconsidered, he could do so by proposing it as an item for a future agenda.

Mme Kegg expresses the opinion that we come together for friendship and for the pleasure of each other's company rather than out of professional duty.

M. Seil speaks standing up, smiling, in the doorway, beside three other smokers. He does not come into the room and his voice carries poorly. People shout at him to speak up.

This commotion disturbs the sleep of M. Tromb who leaps up, raises his hand, wants to say something, begins a sentence, gives up and says it is too complicated so he will let it drop.

M. Anderson insists on the importance, above all, of harmoniously harmonizing the structural structure of the general objectives.

M. Renoti says that we must first establish our philosophy. Do we or do we not have to establish our objectives in the light of the size of our membership and the needs of all?

Mme Vendler confirms that our needs are the basis of everything. First we must identify our needs. She makes that a motion.

Mme Wyck repeats that we are repeating ourselves, that these needs have already been defined by the founders of our brotherhood (as she calls it).

M. Thub protests that questions already raised by the members of this assembly should be dealt with.

M. Renoti asks what questions he means.

He does not get an answer.

M. Brodsky suggests making a distinction between the needs and the desires of the members. One can interpret the word 'need' by what is necessary for a member to attain an objective. And the word 'desire' by what the member would like the league (his word) to do for him. Needs are different from desires. The first word is often wrongly used to signify the second.

Mme Cobb proposes that a survey be made, using a written questionnaire, to establish the needs and desires of everyone in the group, as defined by M. Brodsky.

M. Tytell asserts that such an inquiry would be totally useless. To prepare such a questionnaire, innumerable meetings would be necessary, and a questionnaire of that type would not result in the answers that are wanted. M. Anderson announces an amendment he would like put forward, in the event of a motion being made, to introduce the word 'desire' which seems to him of an importance as important as the word 'need', desire being the desire for desire, and need being the need for need.

M. Tytell finds this distinction totally pointless. Such hair-splitting does not advance the discussion by one step.

M. Brodsky does not agree with M. Tytell and is in fact of the opinion that a third variable ought to be taken into accord:

demand. Demand, as distinct from need and desire, is placed between the two. To make clear what is involved, he invites the assembly to reflect upon the categories of the noun 'lack'. Three levels can be recognized (he goes to the blackboard to illustrate): privation (absence) which is an actual lack; frustration (presence) which is an imaginary lack; prostration (the image of a break in the sequence) which is symbolic lack. Desire is equivalent to privation, need is like frustration, and demand (for mediation, help, support) can be associated with prostration. Prostration is inactive, anti-dynamic. It describes a lifeless state, overwhelmed by lack. Our league is experiencing – only too clearly, according to him – a state of prostration. Thus we may be said to be in the situation of demand. Therefore it is important that this category be added.

M. Tytell admits that he appreciates the intellectual subtleties of M. Brodsky, but he thinks, once again, that such sybilline philosophizings are totally inappropriate under the circumstances. They introduce needless complications. In being over-eager to clarify, people sometimes only confuse. Which is what is happening with us.

M. Janet, on the contrary, thinks these distinctions simplify the matter. There is an important difference between a two-way choice and a three-way choice. If we add a third element, we arrive at the logic of infinity....

M. Anderson insists on the important importance of demand to demand of each member his need for desire and his desire for need, as well as to demand the demands by way of desires and needs of our union (his word).

M. Renoti surprises us by introducing a new idea. If one speaks of the needs-desires-demands of the members of the federation [*sic*], why not also invoke those of non-members? This is a route to be explored with a view to recruitment. In the objectives, this could be taken into account.

Mme Grave isn't too sure if her confusion might be due to her long maternity leave, but she finds that certain speakers lack seriousness, and apologizes for not always understanding certain others.

For Mme Berg, definitions are necessary if demands are to be responded to. That is where we must begin. However, needs are difficult to define because they might be, in fact, externally determined by someone other than the persons considered. Furthermore, our syndicate [*sic*] cannot act to satisfy desires, because they follow fashion and are constantly changing. It would therefore be absurd to introduce them as an objective. One element remains: demand. We must concentrate on that.

Mme Vendler responds with the suggestion that we must take the needs and desires of the membership into account.

M. Thub adds that we should also consult former members, i.e., those who no longer work with us. The reasons for which they left might help us define the three preliminary elements.

Mme Cobb moves a coffee break to clarify our ideas.

Applause.

* * *

After a quarter of an hour the discussion is resumed. According to M. Tromb, the situation is very simple. The direction of the society can only be open or closed. Should we restrict ourselves to one field of endeavour, like, for example, the club SDU (Separated, Divorced, United) or the Association of Men and Women of Suicidal Tendencies (AMAWOST)? Or should we open ourselves to several fields of endeavour, like, for example, the non-profit group Shoreline, which comes to the aid of the city's homeless but also has ecological concerns and interests itself in the totality of human problems? We must choose one direction and not two. Then we can define a philosophy.

Mme Wyck sums up our situation: we are now, she says, coming back to the eternal questions which have always divided our brotherhood [*sic*] in two. There cannot be one single philosophy on these matters. A decision could be made, but that decision would satisfy one group while making the other discontent. Furthermore, we shouldn't enter into competition with other groups like our own. She suggests that we take up – point by point – the report of the Special Committee on General Objectives and that we come to a decision on it.

The president interrupts the order of the speakers. Anyone who wishes to may put forward a motion of censure for this action and he is ready, in that case, to resign immediately, but he thinks it his duty to speak out to underline the fact that the report of the Commission on General Objectives has just been presented. The committee in question was required to present its report at a meeting of the assembly, which assembly has this very evening received and accepted the report. We can't now change our minds. Therefore, let's forget it. Moreover, we possess in our archives a report of the preceding administrative council prepared in the light of its understanding of the issues at the time and written with a view to renewal. Interested persons may consult it at the archives by making an appointment with the person concerned, Mme Kegg.

Once more Mme Wyck takes up the attack. When it was a matter of inscribing one or another of the objectives in the current charter, it was always done in the name of one or another philosophy in the general assembly. To be or not to be open? It's always the same problem. We are repeating ourselves. The question of objectives is always debated with the same division of opinions. She suggests the most recent report of the Commission on Objectives be the jumping-off point for discussion.

Mme Vendler is in favour of this, while also asking that we take account of the figures shown on the blackboard. She emphasizes that the discussions grow longer as the number of members grows smaller. That says something.

Laughter.

M. Thub, climbing onto his desk, his face livid, suggests using the above-cited report as the basis of discussion because it was the conclusion of a long debate of the Special Committee and also because this collective document should contain the elements of a philosophic stance.

M. Tromb, staying in his chair, nods his head and supports this. The report of the Commission provides the rudiments of an analysis of the generalities which can't be ignored. That analysis should form the basis of our deliberations.

M. Tytell, with a half-smile, finds it strange that after hours of debate we are still at the point of asking ourselves what we should be discussing. He requests that this remark go unrecorded because it might discredit us in the eyes of possible readers and especially our successors.

M. Poquey thinks that the circle [*sic*] should organize more dinner meetings.

M. Bone, a new member, says that he has joined our party (his word) in order to launch the ILF, the Idea Liberation Front, and to found a common-front magazine to be called 'The Bond'.

M. Tromb replies that the SDU (Separated, Divorced, United) already publishes a magazine with precisely this title (which is unintentionally ironic): *The Bond.*

Laughter.

M. Thub points out that before worrying about the name of a hypothetical magazine, it seems more important – to him – to change that of our group.

The president rules that question out of order.

M. Tytell would like the last article of the report of the Commission on General Objectives to be read. He asks that it be read aloud and in an intelligible manner, i.e., not too quickly.

The president agrees to reread it.

We learn in this article that the Special Committee proposes its own dissolution as well as that of the association. Now this article, emphasizes M. Tytell, was voted upon, along with the rest of the report, at the beginning of the evening. Therefore the Special Committee no longer exists and our club [*sic*] has committed hara-kiri. All that's left for us to do is to go home.

The president re-opens the discussion by asking the assembly to take into account the fact that despite everything we are here to discuss the direction of the association. He asserts that according to our rules of procedure, a motion that has been voted cannot be debated again during the same meeting. However, following a written notice of motion, it can be at a subsequent meeting.

M. Tytell counters by invoking the total unreality of this workshop. In any case we haven't the money to do anything. Why not try to discuss and resolve this fundamental problem?

Mme Cobb suggests the immediate organization of a 'rockathon' (she explains that this activity consists of rocking in a rocking chair for as long as possible without stopping. Sponsors pay the participants by the hour) to raise funds in order to get some concrete projects underway.

Mme Berg considers that a benefit concert would be more appropriate.

Mme Finn proposes that, instead, we get a calendar made using drawings by woman artists and texts by poetesses, which would reflect the spirit of equality in our mutuality (her word).

M. Seil suggests unisex T-shirts printed with the name of the corporation. To that M. Bone adds the idea of stickers with slogans.

Mme Grave sponsors the idea of, in collaboration with a manufacturer, selling candies.

M. Poquey suggests, recalling a childhood memory, that these candies could look like small red fishes and taste of ginger.

M. Tromb is forcefully in favour of dried banana slices.

M. Thub, his voice choking, choking, grimacing with effort, makes a motion to table the proposal. Such a motion closes the discussion but requires it to be re-opened at a later date. And no arguments are allowed.

M. Brodsky tries to understand what a motion to table is, and how it differs from a motion to adjourn.

The president considers this a very interesting problem, and asks our procedural expert, Mme Kegg, to whisper the explanation in his ear. He turns back to the assembly, now buzzing, and announces: 'No further discussion.'

The motion to table is carried with three abstentions.

The secretary *ad hoc.*

H.G. Stack

***

At the next meeting a motion of censure will be raised with regard to M. Stack, for his work – which was considered fanciful. He is said to have lacked objectivity in the transcription of our deliberations. As a result of this irregularity, a special commission was created to study the possible forms of written communication within the society, with the purpose of standardizing them. The committee's mandate is to define clearly and in detail 'account', 'record', 'Hansard', 'statement', 'minutes', which are all texts of information; 'report', 'collective document', and 'chronicle', which are texts of intervention. Because in the exercise of its functions the association is called upon to receive, to conserve and to produce texts of information and intervention, we will exert ourselves to establish their official rules of presentation, their protocols of production, the statutes regulating by whom they may be signed and to whom they may be sent, and their precise limits.

The Open Cage

DECEMBER 25

Here we are. Why? We don't know. We want to rest. From what? Well, first of all, from the trials of getting here.

It was a dark Sunday in November, soaked with rain. My companion was cursing the bad weather. There's no way, she grumbled. She was right. I agreed. My mind was bogged down in the numb swamp of autumn. I could not even concentrate enough to read an article in the newspaper. Instead my eyes strayed to an attractive photograph of the tropics.

> DESTINATION SUN. ESCAPE
> WINTER
> COME HOLIDAY WITH US AT THE SEASIDE

No, there was no way. For Christmas and New Year. I mean, no way we were going to spend our holidays in the freezing cold. Momo was right. We couldn't take it any more. We had to do something decisive.

Now we have arrived. It wasn't easy. We never before had the money to go beyond our own little neighbourhood. But with a little willpower, what can't you do? When you come down to it, it's all so easy. Economize here and there, a few vaccinations, get your papers in order and make a plan. It's so simple. The proof: here we are. In the South. For the first time in our lives. It was time, as Momo said. To wake ourselves up.

To wake up – in a manner of speaking. The heat here swallows our breath like ether and puts us to sleep in the middle of the day.

This afternoon we were in a taxi which drove us from the airport to the hotel. My eye could hardly keep up with the changing countryside. It had no continuity, you might say, but jerked spastically from one scene to the next, like slides on a screen. One after another I recognized them from the tourist brochures. Perhaps I exaggerate. Or maybe it was an illusion: it's possible and doesn't really matter. With my elbow propped against a suitcase, and Momo (who drank too much on the airplane) dozing on my shoulder, I was proud of our decision. The smell of the sea came through the open windows. Finally a summery life under the open sky was to be ours. The driver was singing. His cheerfulness was carried along by the wind and the rolling waves. This feeling of well-being cancelled out the memory of the months of preparation, the long delays, the tension of the flight, the problems of disembarking: forgotten the rude smokers, the squalling children, the pains shooting through the eardrums while descending, the dull formalities at customs, the exhausting struggle for our baggage, etc., even the exorbitant price of our taxi.

Now we are installed in our home-to-be for the next fifteen days. We had reserved a sea-side room with twin beds. We have only one mattress, but comfortable, and our window looks out on the mountains. This is a famous hotel. There is no hot water. But to tell the truth we don't need it. In this stifling country a cold shower wakes you up, as Momo says.

DECEMBER 26

Yesterday evening we agnostic lovers celebrated Christmas at the hotel restaurant. There was nowhere else to go. Nor could we choose what we wanted to eat: the food is obligatorily local. But that is part of the experience and thus very good. Also, this special feature gets us out of our usual eating habits.

I didn't sleep last night. Doubtless because of my state of total euphoria. Everything here invites us to live each moment to its full intensity (novelty excites, as is well known). It should also be mentioned that our room is above a very popular discothèque. Doors slammed joyously until closing time: three o'clock in the morning. Happily, the noise of these insomniacs didn't affect Momo's sleep.

I hardly had time to doze off when, about six o'clock, it was time for the early risers: golf players and hikers getting ready to leave. I have always wondered where those who neither stay up late nor get up early are supposed to live – perhaps on some other planet.

Towards seven o'clock the smell of breakfast from the kitchens went to our heads. To the point of waking Momo. And since we were both up, we went down to eat before the rush. But the dining room was already jammed and we had to wait.

The great event, on this first day of our vacation, was to take ourselves to the beach. Finally we could joyfully open ourselves to the sun and drink the sweet essence of the elixir of the sea. For years I had dreamed of this frank unfurling of the senses, of tasting this total ecstasy of being that rises and falls with the limpid swells.

First contact with the waves: I was expecting a warm welcome, I met a powerful enemy. Its mindless arms enveloped me in a blind mass of brown water, stones, sand and sticky seaweed. Quickly they raised me up – then they threw me to the bottom.

I was almost swept away. I escaped – miserable and wounded – dizzy with shock, smothered in salt, my skin all scratched, my spine bruised and my toes twisted.

Momo, more prudent, only waded in: a jellyfish bit her: Her sobs and cries of fear quickly attracted a crowd. We learned there had been two drownings yesterday. And I understood why other holiday-makers hardly strayed from the shore.

'DESTINATION SUN...AT THE EDGE OF THE SEA' was indeed what had been advertised in the newspaper.

So be it. We started to make the most of the beach. Like the others. Why insist on being different? Every half hour a small and very picturesque band came to cheer us up for a few minutes; afterwards a charming boy passed the hat. Women in rags constantly offered us home-made cakes, sweetmeats, clothes. We were well taken care of.

Momo spotted some unused beach chairs. We settled down in them to relax. Right away a black beach attendant came up and asked us to pay for our places. Momo got a little annoyed. And with good reason. I refused to pay. Then the man wrote something in his hand, with a pen, right onto his skin.

I got up and saw the blue numbers (those of our room) standing out as clearly as veins on the grey-pink surface of his palm. Our numbered keytag was dangling (the informer) outside my bathing suit. I realized that the cost would automatically be added to our hotel bill. The black man disappeared without even bothering to argue with us.

And so we no longer kept track either of what we spent or what we did. Everyone kept busy, you might say, watching their sweat rise and admiring, in this new miraculous Assumption, how the sun draws from the self and carries away all which is bad.

At dusk, purified and burned, we came back to the hotel. I wrote a postcard to my brother Doudou.

'Here the body – radiant with light, astounded by its own fire, dazzled by its material reality – finally discovers that it exists.

'Momo and Djo.'

DECEMBER 27

Sunburn prevented me from sleeping. Also my numerous mosquito bites, which itch terribly. As well, Momo has been sick all night: nausea, vomiting, diarrhea, blackouts. Nonetheless we took all the necessary precautions (vaccines, quinine, etc.) and we have avoided the tap water and ice cubes. We even brush our teeth in bottled carbonated water (the only pure water available) which is very disagreeable (but we're getting used to it).

Momo has had to consult the hotel doctor (which goes to show how secure we are: even illness has been provided for). He prescribed some medicine to soothe her. A day of rest, in the shade, keeping cool.

Tomorrow we'll escape. To be ready we go to bed early. The humidity has risen considerably and for the first time we have to use the noisy air conditioner.

DECEMBER 28

Our hotel is isolated at the edge of the beach. To reach the nearest village and get a feel for the country takes an hour on foot. Which could be a beautiful walk. Impossible to get lost, there is only one road. We took it.

As we advanced, the tumultuous variety of fantastical plants with their electrical jolts of darkness and light gave way to dishevelled sprays of dried branches. In the distance, the stony mountains melted into the unreality of a mirage. From time to time we would stop to listen. The intense light seemed to strip the landscape of all sound and to thicken the silence.

Once at our destination we found ourselves gawking. Suddenly it was the opposite of exotic. We were now in a vast garbage can of humanity, a maze of straw and cardboard houses where life was lived at a crawl. Seated on their beds of earth, the inhabitants pass their days with their mouths hanging open. Beside them, huge snakeskins dry in the sun. Like the vacationers on the beach.

The praises of the market had been sung to us. It was a confused mass of flesh, an odorous display of shells, dismembered animals, whole skins. And the manure, here, smells exactly the same as at home.

About turn. We go back. Cold shower. I send a card to my parents.

'This village balances proudly on a cliff. The houses are fragile. Not for them the dark and heavy life of our stone dwellings. Surrounded by mist and heat these habitations seem to want to melt into a dream. Under the beating sun, colours run and mix, both objects and living beings lose their exact definition. The richness of this destitute place where every hour is like every other and the moment expands to push back the borders of time.

'Momo and Djo.'

DECEMBER 29

My turn for stomach flu. It's everywhere so it had to be expected.

Here, the digestive process is a newsworthy subject and nourishes the daily conversations. At table you can – without risk of seeming impolite – ask a stranger: 'By the way, are you having intestinal problems?'

We bought sunglasses to protect our fatigue-ridden eyes. Attempts to read beneath the palms. Impossible: too much light. Attempts to daydream, but the mind is numbed by the heat. Leaving stupor. Nap to the droning of insects. Privilege of holidays: to have enough time before one to experience the pleasure of wasting it.

In the evening, in our room, I hastily scribble a note to my sister Clio:

'I often see children wearing strange giant seaweeds shaped like trumpets. In these trumpets I can recognize the symbol of approaching paradise. A heathen paradise to be sure. That says it all.

'Momo and Djo.'

DECEMBER 30

Wind, night. The sea tosses. The waves roar like engines. Insomnia. Rise early. Organized excursion into the hinterlands.

Into the desert, in fact. There is not a single human trace to be seen: road, fence, house, smoke ... The horizon dissolves into the mirage of a trembling expanse of water. There, the world seems to end in a luminous wave. The eye is lost in it and can no longer see. Momo understands this, she is quickly put to sleep by it.

But I believe that in this void I have discovered something like the feeling of true freedom. Here the mind feels entirely clear and space is restored to all its grandeur.

I spent half the night hunting a small lizard that frightened Momo and almost kept her from sleeping.

DECEMBER 31

We finish the year with the whole group. At the hotel restaurant of course. New Years' Special: dinner and dance. We are allowed to eat as much as we like of any of the local dishes which we have been eating since our arrival.

Cries of joy, flutes and rattles herald the arrival of midnight. We end up with confetti on our plates, paper hats on our heads, blow-out feathered streamers beneath our noses. Balloons burst in our faces and, under the tables, chains of firecrackers machine-gun our legs. We leave.

Outside, it's the fireworks display in the night sky. Luminous tumult of exploding rockets: polyps of brightness, cornucopias of stars, glowing showers of sparks slowly falling. People wandering on the beach, wanting to prolong this moment of intensity.

Suddenly a whistling across the emptiness. It lands on me: a cartridge explodes. They're throwing firebombs at us! Juvenile delinquents probably. We withdraw from all this hyper-activity and, a little further on, we are entwined in the cool sand to wish ourselves a Happy New Year. Just as I embrace Momo a boot buries itself in my back. Some drunk has stumbled over us and now begins to swear and curse. He even wants to fight with me.

All night we hear firecrackers exploding and bottles breaking against the rocks.

JANUARY I

Late in the morning. At the dawn of this New Year, after shaving, I felt more affectionate and more demonstrative than ever. I searched for some loving and eccentric thing to do for Momo: with her lipstick I wrote a too-banal 'I love you' on the mirror above the sink. Just like in the movies! I had always dreamed of doing this and the disorientation of travelling must have given me courage. I went back to bed, waiting for Momo to wake up. Quivering with excitement I imagined her surprise.

In fact she was very upset with what I'd done and scolded me because I had ruined her lipstick, which was very expensive. She was right, I hadn't even given a thought to that problem.

At the end of the afternoon we timidly decided to imitate the crowd of well-behaved and joyful tourists who, every day at the same time, toned up their bodies with a brisk run along the beach.

But we were unprepared for such exercise and had to stop. We should at least have had the appropriate footgear. Momo hurt her foot on a shard of glass in the sand. Doctor, bandage, everything. From now on, we would have to avoid walking.

Chance encounter with a couple of elderly compatriots. The man tells us that he has lost his dentures while trying to swim. He can no longer eat solids. Because of this emergency they have cut short their stay and are going home tomorrow. They were lucky, they tell us, they got the last available seats on the airplane for a week.

We are condemned to this holiday: all action suspended; time stopped; the river of life frozen.

I am sending a postcard to Momo's parents. I will be careful, in order to keep them from worrying, not to say anything about the accident.

'This is a country where the foam-washed beaches stretch out to infinity. And while following stitch by stitch the whole delicate trail of this lacework of sand – it's the hem of the earth's skirt dipped in the sea – you finally arrive at the absolute: the wonder of here.

'Momo and Djo.'

The Secret Voice

A VOICE. Which shattered language. Deliciously. A foreign voice, which said: 'Touch me. I am the skin of time. And I never think. Thought, knowledge, meditation – there are many people still struggling at this level. Let's leave them to it. You and I – we go beyond. There is nothing to understand, my sweet. It is enough to experience. Yes – in feeling is everything. To feel the orifice of the planet open against my mouth. To hold the beauty of our thrilling words and let ourselves reach across the night, with nothing to separate us, SWALK ...'

The voice always whispered this magic syllable, SWALK. Prolonging it. Nonchalantly. Sensually. SWALK: sealed with a loving kiss, is what it meant. The voice taught us to repeat this term. SWALK. Orgasmic provocation of an echo, mutual fulfilment in the same euphoric chaos. It was such an exquisite pleasure to hear that warm intonation. Which seized us, again and again, reconnecting us to life. We girls who had been overeducated, overprotected. SWALK. SWALK. Rare spring of deep emotion to succeed in touching us. We cherished the voice for all the doors it made yield within us.

That voice talked to us over the telephone. It talked to us when we dialed its mysterious number, discovered by one of us. Dream figures, over which we brooded, jealously: our deep secret. The number gave us free access to the forbidden kingdom of that disturbing male voice. Always the same: deep, soft, sweet, sympathetic. A silky evening murmur. Or Sunday afternoon. Waiting at the tips of our fingers. To fill our adolescent emptiness.

That unknown voice hid itself under the name of Albert.

What damp and longing looks, what liberating confessions, what electronic body-to-body, what paradise close to home did Albert offer us?

Should we call him all together? Then, all excited, we would talk to him in turn, amuse ourselves with him by confessing everything and nothing. Some of us innocent, others provocative, we told him about our problems of the moment – mostly imaginary – our loves – in fact nonexistent – or our desires – a mixture of pretence and dreams.

Always the same unfailing welcome. His patience. His politeness. Also his curiosity. His indiscreet questions were encouraged by our confidences. His playful insistence made us important. Albert was interested in the colour of our hair, of our eyes, in the shape of our lips. He solicited precise physical descriptions, the better to construct images around the anonymous voices he was hearing. He murmured our names, invented affectionate surnames for us, decorated them with charming diminutives. Often, with one of us, an intimacy developed, a closeness explicitly sensual. And this was indeed the most titillating. Blushing exchanges, temperatures rising. His man's words sought us out, quietly, never sliding into vulgarity – that would have put us off – and ended, in their distance, by having marvellous effects on us. To us, Albert was a consoling prince. He was giving us therapy through words and making possible our small transgressions. Transgressions that were reassuring because without consequence, yet essential because they were our release.

'Let's get excited, just a little,' he would murmur when, in secret, I could call him alone.

Deeds. Words. Silences. Hypnosis. SWALK. It was better than in books. My body knew itself. The ear no longer paid attention to the understanding of words: hearing lost its head, its normal intelligence went to sleep, the wild talk had no more meaning. It became a kind of probe slid into me, exquisite penetration that left me paralysed with pleasure.

Strong, honest male presence – tender and captivating – it insinuated itself into my silence, numbed me like a venom, caught me in the mesh of its desire. Sugared state of being. Space saturated with exquisite delight. The whole body abandoned to the sensuous pleasure of language, to the languor of sensual pleasure. That sorcerer's voice, carrying me away.

'Sail with me, my little boat, into the wind, come to my smile ...'

And always his desire, tuned perfectly to mine, half-whispered. Sweet murmured invocations of desire.

Memories of drunkenness in his company. Time for serenity and for passion. Time to taste the slow rise of pleasure. SWALK. The long complex awakening of the senses with him, breathless, in the night of the telephone, the glow of darkness. Slipping sensually through surrounding mists. Floating in the stream of his voice, of my own. Mad explosion of flesh in the throat, agonies of separation.

I wasn't playing a role. I was sixteen years old and in love with this voice. I had no idea whose it was. The strongest feelings of my life had only a wire to hang on to. That's how it was.

* * *

In time it evaporated, that so soft voice. But it came back much later, thirty years later, one evening when I discovered by chance, while leafing through an old box of letters, that so exciting number: Albert's.

There it was, the misty sound of love conserved, numbered, among the essential mementoes of my past. SWALK. Sealed with a loving kiss. Explosive fetish still adored for the return of those first thrills that it evoked. And when I told the whole story to my husband, the voice, overwhelming wave, came back more strongly. But did I really remember it, with its whole range of sights, its carefully modulated army of joyous moments, its throatful of secret emotions? The more I repeated the number to myself, the more the old voice notes were reborn, and came together again to replay the harmonies of that scenario of the past.

The inner ear heats up, becomes aroused, hallucinates. The ear knows what it wants, and goes to find it, back there where the old full orchestral score of love is being performed anew. The ear knows and wants that voice with its power to surround so softly, its lulling tones that make the world fall away, and all the erotic vistas that lie beyond.

The temptation was irresistible. My hands fumbled nervously with the telephone. Memory of actions so often repeated. No answer. Relief? Disappointment.

By this event my husband and I were plunged into an unprecedented state of excitement. Because, in this random number, my husband recognized that of one of his childhood friends, Henri, whom he sometimes still saw.

Various theories occurred to us. Might I have been mistaken about the number? That would seem to be impossible, the memory of it was anchored in my flesh itself. Might someone different now have that number? But no, it was in fact the number of Henri's mother, he had always lived there because his father died just after Henri married. Might Henri have played the role of Albert? Unlikely. He would have been too young, because he was the same age as us. While the voice of the unknown man had, in its timbre, the undeniable weight of time. Then who wore the mask of Albert? Lacking any clues, the riddle remained entire and we were left without a solution.

Finally, tired of analysing, interpreting, uselessly examining and re-examining, we lost interest in the story.

***

Then, one summer evening, something happened: we received an invitation that we could not politely refuse – I had to accompany my husband to Henri's house. The story of Albert hardly crossed our minds. Instead we had our appearance to worry about. The occasion was supposed to be formal: the men in black tie, the women in evening gowns.

It was crowded. Most people were standing. Everyone stiffened by the varnish of manners and the cramp of etiquette.

Introductions. Kissing of hands. Meeting of eyes. Disconnected cocktail conversation. Trays heavy with glasses and bottles. Petits fours. The classic display of the total emptiness of fashionable parties.

At a certain moment during the evening, having talked too much, I became aware of an overwhelming thirst (I never take alcohol). I went to the kitchen to get something to drink. Sitting there was Henri's mother, whom I had already met. Beside her, standing, was her maid, a corpulent woman in uniform complete with cap. I asked the hostess if I might have a glass of water. She immediately relayed my desire to her domestic who said, simply: 'Yes, of course, Madame.'

Those four words, however insignificant and natural in their context, stunned me: they had been uttered in a voice abnormally low and I stood there, stupefied, because I was absolutely certain I had just heard the voice of Albert! In a state of shock I accepted my glass of water, trembling, and ran back to my husband. I pushed him out to the terrace, away from everyone else, and told him what had happened. I had been so totally stricken that I was unable to control myself and couldn't even speak without stammering. We had to leave.

***

Afterwards I spent long hours shut up in my apartment, in the circle of a candle's light listening to my favourite operas and my foreign voices, my voices of men. Away from the world.

My husband says I seem like the image of a Madonna, a virgin who has lost her will, contemplating the eternal.

There is nothing to understand, my sweet. Feeling is all. I am the skin of time. And I never think. SWALK.

Believe Me

YOU MAY HEAR certain malicious rumours about me. Don't believe them. I may seem old and crotchety but I'm a good-hearted person, you'll see. I wish I could say as much for our neighbours, who never stop complaining about each other. Believe me, this place has become a Hell. If I didn't have to take care of Benta, I would move. Yes! It's come to that point. That tells you how fed up I am. And also my apartment has become too big for me. Eight rooms for just one person, it's too much. Think of the housework! You know as well as I do that it's impossible to find help these days. And, when you can, it's expensive. And when you can hardly pay your rent, you have to take care of things yourself. I was talking about it the other day with Benta: she says it's the same everywhere.

Poor woman, she's had a hard life. There are days when she would like to die. You know there's little to envy in the job of the concierge. She has this whole building – and the one beside it – on her back. People harass her all the time. Every day brings new problems. She has the garbage cans to take care of, the stairs to clean, the owners and the tenants to keep happy. They're never satisfied. They criticize her all the time, malign her without scruple. It's true. On top of everything else she has to submit to these unjust accusations. They even criticize her for wanting life's little pleasures. Imagine! She doesn't claim to be a saint, but all the same! Listen to them for a few minutes and you'll see. You know the old story: do nothing, everyone complains; do something, they scream. You might as well just go through the motions.

Just the same, if this building is respectable and well-maintained, it's her we have to thank. I can assure you, I know something about it. It's heartbreaking to see her devotion to these ingrates. After all the trials she's been through, it's inhuman to treat her this way.

It's true that sometimes she goes about things the wrong way. Her frankness and her spontaneity don't always make her likeable – it has to be admitted. That creates tensions. And I, in all that – I have a difficult position – between a rock and a hard place, you understand. And believe me, they rub it in.

The other day, Monsieur Clem who lives on the third floor said to me, 'You've lost your dignity. You have such a beautiful apartment there on the second floor, I don't understand why you are living at the concierge's. It's unseemly.'

But I get along well with her, and so what? What harm can it do? The important thing isn't where you are but how you feel. No? You don't think so?

'But she's just a concierge,' Monsieur Clem continued. 'Between you and her is a gap –'

So? Benta and I – we can spend hours talking: she never bores me. That woman has been through so many things! It's amazing! She has not had an easy life.

Just as you would think, things went downhill after her divorce. The children, all grown, left right away and refused to have anything to do with her. What ingrates children are today. Fortunately I don't have any.

Monsieur Clem from the third floor has got Benta down as a lesbian. You know something? It's true that Benta attracts all sorts of insults to herself. She does it on purpose: she smokes cigars, dresses like a man, etc.

To show you just how provocative this woman is – and also how absolutely astonishing – I'll tell you something else: she used to be a truck driver. Oh, yes. When her husband left her, she found this job right away – and she liked it. For two years she travelled the roads at the steering wheel of a tractor-trailer. You can picture her, with her weightlifter's build and her man's face, her hair cut short – like that – at the wheel of a sixteen-tonner. Incredible, she is incredible. Add to that her deep voice: you can just hear her at the crossroads, yelling at the Sunday drivers.

So, naturally, it's sometimes hard to tell what sex she belongs to. And that's what bothers Monsieur Clem from the third floor, the lover of classification (he works at the zoo). Why do people always want to know what sex they are dealing with? Is it important? What do you think? Myself, I don't believe it's necessary. This blurring of sexual roles, they say, disturbs a lot of people. But they're wrong. You have to keep up with the times. These days there's no point in continuing to go into a swoon over nothing.

It's also been said – by Madame Cauche from the fourth floor – who lives across from the Gabriellis – that she is one of those negative people always looking for what's wrong. One day Benta had to go to Madame Cauche's apartment to look over some plumbing problems, and while she was there she commented on some of those nice things Madame Cauche has. And, can you believe it, Benta managed to spot an invisible crack in an expensive piece of china. Madame decided to be insulted, and hasn't forgiven her.

While we're at it, speaking of Madame Cauche, did you know that she was broken into last week? Fortunately, the robbers didn't take anything; they were looking for money. But they turned the place inside out. And we didn't see a thing! That's just to let you know the kind of danger there is all around us. The Gabriellis had their door reinforced and Monsieur Clem said that you can no longer own things in peace. As for Madame Cauche, she suspects Benta. You can imagine how they're getting along.

Be that as it may, it's true that Benta excels at finding fault. Which can become disagreeable, in the long run; at the extreme, unbearable. Hell is worrying about details. You know it as well as I. But with Benta, things have to be looked at otherwise: her virtues are the flip side of her faults. Due to her love of perfection we have the cleanest entrance and stairways on the street. You have to admit that, at least.

Still, Benta left her job driving trucks to work here. Strange, isn't it, to go like that from one extreme to the other, from a wanderer's job to staying in one place? In fact, I heard that she was fired. Yes. Because one night she had a serious accident: she fell asleep at the wheel (she'd had too much to drink) and must have missed a turn. But that's between us. Please don't repeat it, no one else knows.

You've seen her place. It's tiny, dark, depressing, isn't it? I wonder how she can live here. A little table pushed against a wall, a rickety double bed (her share from the divorce), a stove, a refrigerator, an electric heater. That's all she's got left. Sometimes it amazes me that anybody could be happy with so little. Doesn't it amaze you? Do you know that she often eats nothing but soup? And that she always wears the same clothes: have you seen them? Black pants and sweater, she wears them all week and then again on weekends. She doesn't complicate her life over dressing.

They say that for two years she spent her evenings, in fact her nights (that I couldn't tell you) with her only friend, the superintendant of the building next door, Violetta, that delicate little flower – she must have been in her forties. Violetta always used to wear sunglasses to hide the fact that she was walleyed. When Violetta arrived on the scene she was like a little mouse you wanted to spend the afternoon kissing.

I found out a good one about her. Our Violetta had two children out of a love affair with a monk. Imagine! She had no luck. Her two children killed themselves. That goes to show you: modern life is hard. Violetta had a boy and a girl. Do you know how they died? One night after dinner her daughter, apparently a beauty, said good-night and then went and hung herself in the bathroom. She was twenty-three years old. Surprising, no? Upsetting, you're right. The other one, thirty years old, was married and unhappy: one Saturday he went into a supermarket with his wife to get his picture taken in one of those coin booths. He didn't wait for the film to be developed; while his wife took care of the shopping he went out and killed himself in the car by using a vacuum cleaner hose to bring the exhaust fumes into the interior. The wife went back to the booth and found the strip of pictures – in all four of them he was sticking out his tongue. Can you imagine the state she must have been in? So much for Violetta's children. It wasn't easy for her to accept.

When Violetta moved in, she used to drink a lot and all the time. At least four litres a day. I'm not exaggerating. Once I counted the bottles in the garbage can. I hear she spent years in a drunken stupor. She was trying to forget. Eventually, in the end, she got incurable boils on her neck. She got Benta drinking. You know, when two unhappy people meet, what are they supposed to do? The people in the building hardly appreciated the bizarre couple that they made, and suspected them of homosexuality. They often combined their jobs and shared their tasks from one building to the other. They fought all the time. There were terrible scenes. But otherwise they got along well, it seems, since you could always see them together.

The day of the sad event, I was there. It was the spring. I saw the whole thing. I had met them by chance in the park across the street. I was sitting on a bench, warming myself in the patch of sun between the trees. It must have been a Tuesday, market day. They had both finished their shopping and had come to sit on the grass in the shade.

You don't know how Violetta used to spend. You felt sorry for her in the end. She hadn't a cent but found a fortune to put out on her appearance. Believe me, when she was married, she didn't do without: manicure, pedicure, hairdresser every week. Imagine! That day she had just bought herself some new clothes: a high-necked dress, a dainty little white cape, and a wide-brimmed hat. As though she needed them. She was wearing a fortune on her back and to tell the truth, she looked ravishing. It must have made Madame Cauche jealous. While leaving the building she saw them, and when she came back an hour later, I saw it with my own eyes, she was wearing a hat even wider than Violetta's ...

Benta and her friend were still relaxing in the park. Violetta, singing, had taken off her new shoes and put her hand into her flowered bag to pull out a bottle of red. So right away you understand the kind of picnic they were planning. They passed the litre back and forth and emptied it in a few swallows. And so it continued, bottle after bottle, until, suddenly, Violetta felt sick. She wanted to take off her little white cape, but hesitated. Her actions seemed out of control. She got it half off, put it back on, finally undid it. You could see her face going pale. Benta noticed and told her to eat something. From her bag she took out a package of pralines. Violetta chewed slowly, got up, sat down again, seemed to be out of breath, grimaced with pain.

'Breathe hard,' Benta told her. 'Get all the air you can.'

Violetta, in her bare feet, tried to walk: she staggered and fell into a bush near the fence.

She was drunk, you'll say. I think it was more than that. It looked to me as if she had gone crazy. She was drooling, and hanging on to her big toes as though they were foreign objects. Benta tried to lead her back under the tree. She could only move on all fours. She was regressing. I can still see Benta behind her. From her pocket she had taken out a big red handkerchief, like the ones circus clowns have, and was blowing her nose loudly (she does it without thinking). It must have been a Saturday, after all, my reading day.

Violetta swallowed a few pralines. And opened another bottle. To see them swilling it all down, I said to myself: one day they'll die of it, that's for sure. Someone will discover them dead in the park, or in the street under the wheels of a truck. The wine dribbled on their chins and stained Violetta's dress. I remember it well. Benta helped her clean it with her handkerchief. That detail struck me. She lit a cigarette for her. Violetta smoked, but without inhaling the smoke. After a few puffs she put it out and picked up her things. She had made a good start at walking before she collapsed on the sidewalk.

Benta lost her temper. Her head swung around drunkenly. She swore at her friend. She especially criticized her for falling down. She could have hurt herself.

Benta seemed like a lighthouse, Violetta a frog. To you this image must seem a little strange, but that's how I saw them. I used to write children's stories you know. I guess sometimes it shows, doesn't it? My late husband also published them, thousands of them. Perhaps you've heard of him. He was very well-known. Perkins, he called himself. Perkins, that was the pen name that he used. In any case, it doesn't matter, getting back to my story ... it must have been a Thursday, come to think of it, knitting day. The lighthouse spoke loudly and the frog cried so much she had take off her glasses to wipe her eyes.

The lighthouse offered her some pralines. So they ate the whole package in silence: Benta standing up, Violetta sitting on the sidewalk.

Afterwards, the quarrel broke out again. Benta was shouting so loudly the whole neighbourhood could hear. The frog seemed to be complaining about her sore feet: she had come here to let them rest. She couldn't stand up any more. The lighthouse turned her back on her. Thinking back, it must have been a Friday: I was on my way home from the bank.

Benta, after a moment of calm, helped her friend to her feet. Violetta moved forward slowly, by hops interspersed with pauses. Bit by bit they moved ahead, the lighthouse leading the frog.

Suddenly Violetta crumpled, unconscious. In her fall her sunglasses broke. She wasn't moving. No matter how Benta cursed her, she had to be taken by ambulance to the hospital. She died shortly after.

From cirrhosis of the liver, it seems, complicated by another illness which couldn't be explained. These things happen so quickly. The doctor said she didn't suffer. They always say that.

Benta was the only relation the poor dead woman had in the world. Imagine. So when her death was announced, Benta, you can understand why, went to the hospital right away.

A doctor welcomed her from behind a locked glass door. He absolutely refused to let her in. Because she was badly dressed, dirty and drunk. At least that's what she told me. Incredible, don't you think?

Monsieur Clem says she's dangerous when she drinks. 'What are you talking about?' I asked him. 'She's absolutely harmless, have a heart.' 'You believe what you want to,' he said, 'but getting herself drunk like that, all day long, she disgraces the entire building.'

I don't agree: I've never felt disgraced or humiliated by her. I've always seen these things in a different light than Monsieur Clem, who is very narrow-minded, let me tell you, you must already have realized. If not, you will. Believe me. In Benta's case, we're not talking about the dizziness of weaklings who are unused to drinking and come unbuttoned before dessert. I hate that type, don't you? No, Benta's intoxications are on a larger scale, more suitable to her talent for excess. Think about it a little – the binges she has experienced! And today you might say they have become a necessary part of her volcanic personality. I would go even farther: drink has weathered and shaped her into a human monument. You see what I mean? Occasionally she might be a bit frightening, because the alcohol awakens her extraordinary energies. But I guess you could say I've learned to live with it.

And that day at the hospital, this remarkable woman who does not take no for an answer wished to see the deceased. They tried to stop her but she barged through just the same. How? Well, you won't believe me, right through the glass. I'm not making this up, it's the absolute truth. She broke the glass and, carried away by her rage, cleared herself a path, knocked over the doctor and the guards, all totally stupefied.

She approached the body, wrapped it in her arms and, crying, sat her up in her bed. Then she talked to her, with tenderness but also with anger, as though she were talking to a doll.

Suddenly, in a fit of violent emotion, she lifted up the body and took it away. Some kind of fury was driving her. As incredible as it might seem, she actually succeeded in leaving the building with the dead woman in her arms. As true as life. Everything I'm telling you actually happened. Once more, reality goes way beyond fiction.

Outside, she crouched in the grass at the entrance to the hospital rocking the corpse, and whispered in its ear. For a few moments she'd stroke its head, then smack its face to wake it up.

A doctor approached her. She knocked him out with one punch. Her eyes were popping out of her head. She was foaming at the mouth. She was delirious.

A group of at least a dozen men came to reason with her. They finally succeeded, after a terrible struggle because she resisted so long, in giving her an injection to calm her down.

Now she wants to die too. She's alone in the world. She tries to get back in touch, without success, with what remains of her family: her children. I understand her.

The neighbours sympathize – a little. At my request they've given her some little presents to console her. Me, I do my best to keep her going. I gave her what meant the most to me: my television set. Since then, she has literally adored me. Every evening she invites me to come have a snack with her – and a few drinks. Sometimes I make her treats. I couldn't refuse my company to someone so lonely. We watch television while sipping our wine. Afterwards we talk half the night.

For the time being, she's kept the other building in order to make a bit more money, but she's begun complaining about being overworked. I offered to help her, poor woman. I might seem old and crotchety, but I have lots of time; and these days, time is the most precious commodity. So we go from building to building, sharing the work. Things are easier that way. I'm so busy that I'm hardly ever home any more.

Naturally, this act of compassion has made the people who live here reject me. They've started to think they're above me. That just confirms what I've always thought of them. They say I had a part in this business of Violetta's death. But, you can see, it had nothing to do with me. You can see for yourself how malicious they are. But I have to admit it, what happened to Violetta certainly affected me. You don't forget things like that.

Madame Cauche, in particular, is very hard on me, especially since I made fun of her ridiculous hat. But that one, she is unbearable. Just imagine, the other day she came to see the apartment for rent, just a bit before you, even though she had no intention of moving. You see the type she is. Don't trust her, she's the neighbourhood gossip. She's started to tell stories about me. She cannot bear that 'an upstairs lady' – as they say here – spends her time on the ground floor with the concierge. What harm can it do? You tell me. It gives Benta some company and, in that way, perhaps I can help her to drink less. Without her noticing. A bit at a time. What do you think?

To me you seem very understanding. I think we're going to get along well. You're leaving? In any case, Madame Olivier, I should let you go now because I have to finish cleaning the stairs today.

***

Madame Cauche, you surprised me, how are you today? Do you know, I just met Madame Olivier, the new tenant on the third floor. Not so friendly, you know, if you don't mind me being frank. She never says a word and she listens to you without seeming really to listen ...

The Directions

YOU SEE, what you're asking is not easy to explain. Because this entire edifice is extremely complex. Even its conception required enormous intelligence. In fact, its architecture was entrusted to foreigners who had to be very well paid. I won't reveal their names to you, no point, but professionals on their level – there aren't many, you can believe me. Why do you think someone like me was taken on, permanently, at the information desk? Obviously because this ultra-modern building is the height of sophistication. We are talking about a veritable labyrinth: I have no other word to describe the intelligence of this construction, terribly intelligent, too intelligent.

To get to any part of the building, and more particularly to the precise place you are looking for, you would almost need, my dear sir, to be initiated into the secrets of the entirety of the structure. I have spent an infinite amount of time trying to grasp it. And I have been working here since the inauguration of the building. That would be five years. So you can imagine how many people I've found wandering around lost, and not simple-minded people either, I assure you. You quickly learn to spot in visitors' faces who will get lost and who can manage. But I won't keep you any longer. I know you're in a hurry, of course. So I'll tell you right away and show you the place where you want to go. Follow my instructions carefully and you won't have any problems.

Here they are: go first towards the right and ... you see the first door over there on the left? Good. Ignore it. Instead, concentrate on the one right beside it. Have you spotted it? That's the one you take. When you do, you come into a big empty place without furniture: it's called the Room of Lost Steps. Don't ask me why: I don't really know myself. Sometimes it's used for academic colloquia. In which case it's suitably fixed up, furnished and those who come in are carefully screened. The most eminent conference-goers in the world congregate there. Important business is transacted. Big decisions are taken. I am well placed to know about them. You have no idea of the importance of that hall, so insignificant it appears as you cross it. Don't let yourself be fooled by the mess you see there right now. They just had a congress there, it finished last night. They've started to take the things away, but of course there hasn't been time to clean up. You'll have the disagreeable impression of being in a theatre after a play, in the midst of scenery being dismantled. It's huge, you'll see that for yourself, to the point of causing vertigo and confusing your sense of direction. So I should advise you to be careful: as soon as you enter that room, you must think of only one thing – crossing it quickly and walking forward in a straight line. It's very simple. But forget yourself for one second and you're lost; and you don't know where that might get you.

Have you understood? Once in the Room of Lost Steps you direct yourself towards a majestic blue double door. You can't help seeing it. As a joke we call it the Entrance to Paradise. That's because of the colour. You can't miss it. Hurry to get to this door and open it. You'll find that the doorway with the heavenly name in reality opens on a shadowy corridor. Follow it, sticking to its L-shape, until you get to a series of twelve identical doors – six on each side. Stop at the fifth door on the right, fifth door on *the right,* you follow me? That is, the one before the last one. We call it the Quintessence. Don't ask me why. The fifth – it's easy to remember: think of the five senses or of the body's five limbs (arms, legs, head).

The fifth, have you got that? Be careful, don't make a mistake. Because the door beside it, the fourth, leads to the communal offices for printing, reprography, cacography, idiography – there are so many of them and they're so varied, I don't even know them all myself. Frightening, that place, an incomprehensible tangle and, as well, a veritable Hell of machines so noisy you could go deaf. Anyway, the people there are too busy to bother with you. One day a man who was lost fainted right in the midst of that place. His sudden weakness was due to an excess of fatigue. Which could happen to anybody. Anyway, it took a long time before he was noticed. Can you imagine the scene? I'm telling you: the workers in these services are totally absorbed in their machines. Their tasks demand the utmost precision. They are practically prisoners of their machines. You cannot, you understand, ask them to devote themselves entirely to their work and, at the same time, take on the burden of unexpected visits. On that subject, in any case, they have strict orders. So that's why they'll leave you to yourself if you should end up there. Unless they decide there's something suspicious about you, in which case an extremely disrespectful reception awaits you, believe me. In brief, I've said enough to convince you not to confuse the fourth door with the Quintessence, as we call it.

As for the sixth, it's even worse: it leads directly to the lower floors and the uninteresting world of the boiler rooms. There we are talking about a place which is totally inhuman and, you must instinctively know, forbidden to the public. Should you end up there by mistake you risk, on the one hand, getting trapped in the mazes, in an inextricable network of giant pipes; on the other hand, if you are discovered, you will be immediately arrested and interrogated – indeed knocked around – and all for nothing. You don't believe me? You think I am exaggerating? Just try to put a foot in there ... My friend, it's your business, but it's a waste of time and energy, I assure you. The fifth door, that's all you have to keep in mind, not the fourth or the sixth.

Not the third either: that one protects the domain of the superintendent. He is on the job all year round, without ever taking a vacation. What a curious man! You might be tempted to call upon his services. If so, you should be warned ... come closer, if you don't mind, I don't want us to be overheard ... Don't expect any help from him. Especially on his own territory. So far as work goes, the union limits it to the management of the building's garbage cans. One function and that is all. It stops there. Don't ask anything else of him. Not even directions. He won't tell you.

Why? Because he would be trespassing on my own department and an entirely justified grievance would be landed on him the next day. Better to avoid disturbing him and causing us problems. If you knock at his door, you will be almost automatically implicated in an unfortunate incident. You'll do as you please, but in warning you I am only doing my duty.

The fifth, the fifth: that is the one you should be interested in. Before getting there the second might intrigue you because of the stifled noises you'll hear if you go close. On the other side is a luxurious salon which is the private preserve of the upper echelons of the enterprise and which they use for mysterious meetings. It's impossible to get in: you have to know the code. You'll probably want to press your ear against the keyhole to try to hear what they're talking about: it won't work. Everything is padded precisely in order to prevent the risk of indiscretion. All that can be heard is a meaningless vague murmur of voices. There is no point in lingering there. I am only giving you these details because you are in a hurry, to save you as much time as possible.

Certainly you will have more questions about the first of the six doors, I can see it in your face. I think I can see you imagining all sorts of possible functions, more or less likely. It has a special importance in your eyes because you will pass it before any of the others, which is normal; and also because I am speaking about it last, not an insignificant point. But I'm afraid you'll be disappointed because, in fact, the first door is totally without importance. Behind it is only a cupboard. You would never have guessed it, right? Some people like to pretend that storage place actually contains – now behave yourself – the building's safe. Nothing could be less certain, I assure you. A lot of people worry themselves over this treasure, and everyone has his own version of the truth. I could tell them to you in detail if you like, but let us not abandon ourselves to the pleasures of digression; back to the important point – behind that first door, a place without exit.

So let us return to the fifth. That is the one you must remember. You will use it. It opens, you will see, onto a small corridor crossed at right angles by another corridor. After a few steps (twenty perhaps, actually a little more, about thirty, in any case, you'll count them for yourself) having arrived at the crossing of the second passage, you'll go the left. Careful! Not the right! That is the administration: you will have problems and so will I. They wouldn't hesitate to accuse me of having encouraged you to go there without authorization. But there is a very charming person there, a woman no longer a girl, the secretary of the director general. If ever you should see her, say hello to her from me. She will appreciate that sign of refinement. Nonetheless she has what is, under the circumstances, a slight fault – she likes to talk. So, given your pressing business, be sure to turn to the left. Next you will come to the first large archway. Just beside it you'll see numerous smaller doors. Don't let yourself be drawn to them, they are just offices. Through the archway you'll find a staircase. Bizarre, but that's how it is. I've already told you, this building is absolutely amazing. You go upstairs. When you've reached the top, look to the right. You'll notice two enigmatic doors, also painted blue. They too are called the Doors of Paradise but for different reasons. The one on the right opens out, after a pathway too complicated to explain right now, to a raised terrace. I would take you if you wanted: the view from there is unique. It takes in the city and even, when the weather is good, the near suburb in its entirety. It's worth the effort. But because of your pressing needs, you will certainly go directly to the door on the left. There, finally, you'll find what you're looking for: the rest room. My late mother used to call it 'the room of dreams'. How right she was!

Perhaps you would like me to summarize? Briefly? Okay. Second to the left; next, Door of Paradise, opposite; fifth to the right; first large archway to the left; up the stairs, right, and finally left. So go. I hope you've got it. Don't hesitate to ask me to repeat it if there is something you don't understand. Or come back to see me if you don't find it. I am here to clear up mysteries, that's my function. But I think that you'll manage, I can see it in your face. And also I understand your impatience, I know what it is to feel that way. So go now, and good luck! And, once again, come back to see me if you find it.

Exaltation

YOUR HONOUR,

I love the soft availability of things, the goodness of day poured over desire, the green sharpness of naked bodies placed before white walls, the fitting-together of voices when they touch, the quivering yellow of the present, corollas opened near trembling branches and the tender intimacy of stones.

I live in the land of expenditure, and I love its moving floor, foundation of all wings.

Do you see here the seagulls magnetized by the earth? And there the hilltops peopled with tiny riots?

Do you hear the sad and husky cry which is the call of the heights?

That is my land, the Land of Enlightment.

Yes, Your Honour, I work there.

I especially love manipulating inert matter, it does not struggle beneath the blade. And I like going to the holes in the deep bed-rock of the planet to flush out fundamental truths.

I live beyond the point of no return, in a dream of green commas, a faraway headquarters of light, given over to the favours of fire, by the isolated mountain where all roads lead to the open sea.

Everything there is easy, and neverending.

I have no address there, Your Honour, but that means nothing, you know, it's unsurveyed territory, an elsewhere of transparences, a land of blurred horizons, within reach of mirage, with no landmarks other than its sea, no borders save the foam along its shores and the full emptiness of its sky.

It is also a country of reaping and of rapture, where desire abandons itself to long soft satisfaction in the heart of silent complicitous vegetation.

Do you see over there the obscene tide granting the push of the masts and the swell of the sails? Everywhere it's the rage of nakedness, the storm of lust, the search for night, the deflowering of all fruit.

Why are you laughing? I am not waxing flowery for the fun of it. I am not testifying here as a tourist, ladies and gentlemen, I am speaking about my actual life, white-hot, in the vertigo of freefall and maintained at its own height, far from the call of desire and the slurp of the everyday, from the mists of mystification and the ridiculous parade of passing problems, far from the proprieties, restrictions, measurements, far from the common rhythms and mechanical birth of concepts.

I speak to you of a flexible thinking, I speak to you of an existence ever-moving, founded on the leap which blurs all walls and boundaries. This thought is alive: it dances, it turns, it springs forward, it stops, starts again, crosses, goes beyond, deploys. Is deployed.

It follows its own blood. It moves in its own direction.

He who breathes at these heights, Your Honour, sparkles. And he lives – if he can be said to 'live', for time itself is forgotten there – at each instant he lives and experiences the strong brilliant taste of the universe itself.

There the innocent flesh washed by the day, lives in ease, at its ease, electrified in the shade of the magnetized palms, or in the dripping sun wiping away its watery dreams. Or again it walks, necessary radar in the confines of the possible, the long trembling lip of the sea kissing every step, exciting every step, and from its millions of mouths tempting him with its salacious saliva.

In this beautiful affluence of space, Your Honour, it is often just a matter of looking – without even making an effort to speak – and of listening with a certain concentration to the power of what is given – for all to become clear.

Have you ever opened yourself to the possibilities of the outside, without wanting to obtain, to dominate or to undo – but simply to exalt? That is what I do, Your Honour. I wander without purpose, vibrant in the luxury of light, in view of whatever. Let what may become of me, let the dust of every nation settle on my clothes. You see!

Have you felt led to a doorway you cannot find, perhaps two steps away, which will send you into exile if you cross it? That is what has happened to me. I travel into that which cannot be found and nothing can stop me. I always escape: that's my motto. I always seek the new direction, light of foot, free of mind, eye on the horizon, going towards the beyond, farther, ever farther, drunk on the out-of-doors, beyond the confines of these insignificant buildings, from step to step, through valleys and mountains, ever upwards, higher, higher, to the furthest reaches, beyond reality, across mere matter, faster, faster, to finally spurt forth at the end of the race, perhaps lost but in fact arrived, splattered with the void, amazed, blown away, with the sky's blue in my hair and with my sole companion the power of light. If necessary, that is how far I am willing to go, Your Honour.

That supposes vigilance and labour, perhaps danger. I'm prepared. I am fearless. Here in the headquarters of nowhere I sweat away at my rockpile. While all around the mountain peaks doze in the midday sun, I watch over them, I watch over them all the long hours.

While ever more and vaster strokes of brilliance open wide my eyes, my mouth, my notebook.

I write and I write and I write – pages and pages – to my dead family and my lost relations. Take care! That does not mean no one. I talk to them about my friends, my otherworldly, timeless friends who are men without profession, men of the sea or desert, men of the sun: this gypsy blowing his harmonica to the rhythm of his mules, that dreamer dangling from his tip of land, this storyteller whitened by the dusty road, that collector of agates and shells, this searcher of trails into the infinite, that lover of paths lost or sharp perfumes, this seeker of pleasure who spends his days in scented gardens washing human bodies, caressing them, polishing them like stones or shining ornaments.

I speak to them of my friends of straw, of my friends with open hands. To them I also tell of my pagan land where the flame burns, where struggle reigns eternal, where life is on fire, vision enlighted, deeds carved in gigantic stone. To them I describe this elsewhere that welcomes and suffices, where everything demands to be known, where enlightenment in triumphant chorus invites us to freedom, to joy, to the experience of ...

***

LOCK HIM UP.

The Locks

BARTHELEMY is in the huge changing-room of the factory, between two rows of tall metal lockers. On his rolling table can be seen a box of closed locks and a large open book with long columns of figures.

Following numerous complaints of theft, the administration decided to buy 512 combination locks (which will make keys unnecessary) for the 512 lockers in the room. The chosen model has, of course, a steel hoop and a round black metal housing, on top of which, in the centre of a numbered dial, is a rotating arrow (which in some way activates the opening of the lock if moved in accordance to a secret code of three numbers).

For a week Barthelemy put on the combination locks, distributing them according to a pre-established plan. It was a job which required constant attention. These moving locks all look the same, but as Barthelemy quickly realized, each has its own personality and its little sensitivities. The opening depends on the correct execution of the series of three numbers according to predetermined manoeuvres. For example, if his book shows for lock number B2119 the following combination: 34-17-18, that means: a turn to the right up to 34 exactly, a complete turn to the left back to 17, then turning back to the right to 18. One small fraction of an error is enough to make the mechanism balk, and then everything has to be started over.

At the beginning Barthelemy secretly amused himself by turning the central arrow and listening, ear pressed against the works, to the faint clicking of the rings and gears inside. Eventually he grew bored with that.

In his notebook, Barthelemy is supposed to be registering his work. For example, lock C3612, with its secret combination 21-4-19, corresponds to locker 283. And that in conformity with the columns headed respectively:

SERIAL NUMBER, COMBINATION, and LOCKER.

In this manner Barthelemy spent a whole week furnishing each of the 512 lockers with its individual lock. His fingers grew bloody. But he is very proud of his accomplishment.

It is hardly two days since he finished this colossal job, and now he has received the absolutely unexpected order, from another department of the administration, to take off all the locks he so patiently attached. Why? First because all the lockers must be shifted in order to allow extensive repairs and redecorating in the dirty and depressing room where they are kept. Secondly, because these renovations will also provide an opportunity to restore and repaint the lockers themselves. After months of procrastination and studies of all kinds, the architects' plans have finally been accepted. And the workmen will be coming in two weeks.

Barthelemy therefore takes his task to heart and devotes another whole week to removing all the combination locks from the 512 lockers.

Thirty-eight right, 12 left, 17 right; 24 right, 9 left, 13 right; Barthelemy works with such minute attention to detail that he succeeds, every single time, in making the mobile mouth of the apparatus release the bolt and elegantly open. Finally, with a twist of the wrist, he turns the lock, slips it out of the hinge on the locker, delicately sets the open lock in his box. Delicately, so it does not close again: he knows he will have to put it back and does not want to have to reopen them all.

This sequence is repeated 512 times in front of the 512 identical lockers.

A trained team of heavily-muscled movers, using a metal cart, then transport the compartments one by one to a part of the building's basement where specialists in such matters attend to the long overdue repairs. In a notice posted for the workers, the administration apologized for any inconvenience caused by these renovations, which would be concluded within a month.

***

Two months later, the factory workers were still without their cloakroom. They still had to change wherever they could, and leave their personal affairs in any corner they could find. Thus city clothes are found piled up here and there, exposed to industrial dust and dirt. One morning, the men finally reacted, as was to be expected, and complained to the owners.

They, in turn, went to the contractor and asked for an explanation. The renovations to the lockers had not even begun, and the changing room was still in a shambles. The results of the enquiry came out quickly: due to lack of personnel and rising costs, it had been impossible to meet the original schedule. So, fearing a strike, the administration decided to suspend operations and hire a different company. While waiting until they could find a company that would charge a reasonable rate, they had the lockers put back where they had been so that the workers could use them.

Following this, Barthelemy was told to replace the 512 locks according to the plan he had already used. Being the perfect employee, he at first tried to follow the administration's instruction to the letter. But, as the locks were simply heaped in his box, he quickly saw that to try to locate them by their number to make them correspond to the proper locker constituted an absurd and inhuman labour, which would daunt even a more stubborn person than himself, if one could ever be unearthed. Therefore, without breathing a word to anyone, he calmly started the entire operation from zero again. In fact, no better solution offered itself.

So there he is, every day, in a corridor of the changing room with his wheeled table, sometimes bent over his notebook to read a number or to write down new ones, sometimes searching through his box of locks or manipulating the locker hinges, sometimes going back and forth from one to the other to check and check again. His motions repeat themselves, superimpose themselves. Hoop A5869 goes to locker number 408 and, with a blow of the palm, is locked into its housing. Barthelemy notes it in the appropriate column of identification. And so forth for the 512 doors.

As soon as this task is complete, he proceeds to the official assigning of space to the workers and gives to each a small stub on which he writes the combination.

***

Six months later the new contractor arrives. He has received permission to have all the lockers taken to a special warehouse where they will be entirely rejuvenated. Estimated time required: one month. The workers are informed. They immediately object. After negotiations it is decided only half the total number of lockers will be restored. When this is complete the rest will be sent away. Thus the men can at least double up to share space for their clothes. It's better than nothing.

Following this agreement, Barthelemy receives the order to take off all 512 locks and to reassign every second one to the remaining lockers. This time, summoning up all of his courage, he dares to protest to the management. 'To my way of thinking,' he states, trying to impress with his reasonable approach, 'I could simply take off 256 of the locks (the first 256) and give each worker concerned (those without lockers) the combination, which he will have to share with his colleague.'

His argument was immediately convincing. He was even congratulated for having thought of it.

Chest swollen with pride, Barthelemy returned to his rows of lockers: 21 right, 6 left, 10 right; 38 right, 3 left, 17 right. The organism controlling the moving steel hoop held no more secrets for Barthelemy. His movements had a somnambulist's precision. The comparison was his own. It was because he dreamed about it all night. For fear of being laughed at, he didn't tell anyone. But in his bed he twisted and turned from side to side with his head full of numbers, as though his body itself was the axis that controlled the opening.

To replace the codes of the men without lockers, Barthelemy had to locate, in the appropriate column of his notebook, the locker numbers (because, of course, they weren't in order) and mark the new attributions with an x.

Seeing that all these signs began to grow confused, he retranscribed them further along in his book.

***

At the end of fifteen days, as planned, the dilapidated lockers were replaced by their renovated sisters. This operation took up almost a week. During this time the factory workers were again without a changing room. As for Barthelemy, he was entirely occupied in taking off the 256 locks that remained. He could hardly keep up the pace, the team of movers was so efficient.

The 256 restored lockers were now lined up: all had been painted blue and shone with cleanliness. Barthelemy, with an unspeakable inner joy (which he hid from the others for fear – again – of seeming ridiculous), decided the whole process had been worthwhile and the job totally successful. This happy feeling made him well-disposed to attempt the replacement of the 256 new locks. Eagerly he set himself up with the wheeled table. Then he discovered a problem, one which not only killed his enthusiasm but also sent him into deep depression. The exterior metal of the lockers had been spray-painted, wiping out the numbers of the lockers so that it would no longer be possible to match up the lockers with the appropriate lock.

Trembling, he went to inform the administration. Because he might be held responsible for this careless mistake. And in fact he was poorly received. They pronounced themselves tired of being bothered with these trifling details. They told him to take care of his responsibilities and to manage as best he could. He had only to scrape clean the little plaques in question and the problem would be solved. But the workers? What about the workers? They will have no lockers. Very well, let them use the cloakroom as it is for the meantime, that's all.

Barthelemy did as he was told. For another week it was total chaos: men came and went, mixed with the renovators. Barthelemy, precariously perched on a rickety step-ladder, applied himself to removing the paint from the 256 minuscule sprayed plaques. In accomplishing this duty he quickly noticed that the lockers had not been re-installed in their proper numerical order.

After much hesitation, to the point of being unable to sleep, he finally decided to alert the administration. This time the problem was judged to be a serious one. The foreman was advised of this unfortunate error and charged with putting things back in order without delay. It took 48 hours before all the compartments had been replaced, in their correct order, under the strict personal supervision of Barthelemy.

Next, without waiting for further instructions, Barthelemy re-immersed himself in the epic of the locks, following the same principle he had previously outlined to the management: 256 combination locks and 256 combinations to be distributed among 512 workers, two at a time. All this was entered into his fourth column – LOCKER – in his book. There, everything seemed clear and precise, despite the complexity of the thing.

***

The renovations in the room were completed when the missing half of the lockers arrived. The plaques, this time, were intact, specific instructions having been given to the painters. Everything was arranged in numerical order. This Barthelemy oversaw himself. It was in his own interest. The changing room now had eight rows of 64 lockers. It was a masterpiece of balance and uniformity.

But Barthelemy did not take the time to admire the beauty of this ensemble: he was more preoccupied with the well-being of the workers, and the administration was pressing him. His final problem was to effect the redistribution of the locks to the 512 lockers. In order to ensure that each had its secret combination, he first had to take off the 256 shared locks that were already in place. That was self-evident. He saved much time and energy by assuming his full responsibilities and using his ingenuity: in this spirit he decided to switch all the locks from one row with those opposite. Why hadn't he thought of it before? This symmetrical exchange concerned only three rows. In the first corridor he methodically proceeded with the first step: he opened all the locks on both sides and let them hang in place.

Satisfied with having invented this system, and happy with the first stage, he went to boast to his co-workers during coffee break. While he talked some practical jokers went to shut all the locks he had just opened. Back from his break, Barthelemy saw the stupid trick that had been played on him and began to weep. Just a few tears to help himself unwind. His hands were covered with blisters from turning and re-turning the arrows. He couldn't go on. If this continued he would have a nervous breakdown. But there was no choice. He bent himself to his task once more, opening again his locks and quickly changing them, from locker to locker, this time as he went along. Next he quickly wrote down, two by two, the number of the lockers in his fifth column LOCKER. Until he had done the 192 doors of the first three rows.

Endless day after endless day, he communed with his wheeled table and took care of the remaining lockers: placing upon them their locks, writing down the number of the plaque in the notebook. Finally to each worker he was able to give his own locked compartment. But he must have made an error somewhere, either in recopying the combinations while putting everything back in its correct order, or in switching the locks from row to row, because the men were no longer able to open their combinations.

The director was informed. Barthelemy was ordered to do the

necessary to rectify his error. He succeeded in spotting the problem by carefully reading and re-reading the multiple columns and comparing them with the versions he had copied out, as well as checking the transfers he had made in the first three rows. He had skipped a line in the transcription of the codes and that inattention had entirely ruined his system.

That accomplished, Barthelemy received the order to take off all the locks (their serial numbers allowing him to know their combinations) and to sell one to each of the workers.

Having taken that decision, the administration had no further need of Barthelemy and fired him.

A few days later a small party was organized to celebrate the opening of the new changing room and to thank the workers (whom the managers tactfully termed 'collaborators') for their patience during the renovations.

All Aboard!

IN THE COUNTRY, one summer morning, I ran out of my house searching for the right word. That had often happened to me lately. But this time, the thing had reached worrying proportions. I could not remember the words for the most elementary activities around me, and I felt that I would henceforth be incapable of identifying, classifying, configuring – in brief, calling things by their names.

Suddenly I was in a universe in total abandonment to the void, and I took an astonished step backward in my relations with reality. For quite some time I was plunged into anguish. Some would call that a depressive state. These things come upon us without our fully realizing. We no longer know how to set one foot in front of the other, we don't know where we're going, who we are, what we have done in this life, we seek somewhere to begin, we become blank and as if transparent. That's what happened to me.

My training in philosophy had taught me the verbal mastery of the world. Now, in a single moment, the essence had escaped me, and presented itself as a closed system. Hair dishevelled, face smooth, lips electric, I saw myself become stupid and unable to think. This impotence seemed so unlike me. To get out of it, I trusted to my senses, following an old habit that had helped me out of many a difficult situation in the past: I inhaled the atmosphere to measure the degree of its reality; used my nose and filled my lungs with the morning air; moistened my index finger with saliva, pointed it towards the sky to study the direction of the wind. Some gymnastics to quicken the circulation: fifteen movements of the legs, fifteen of the torso, fifteen of the arms; that is enough to oil the mind and wake up awareness (it doesn't need much, I know).

After this little ritual I tried, as I always do in crucial moments such as these, to engage myself in a special meditation of the landscape, which I sum up in a single infinitive: to-be-open. Every setting conceals a personality that gives it accent and meaning. To-be-open is a way of inner recharging through strolling about which, for a certain time, puts me in a state of awareness of the out-of-doors. To-be-open consists of experiencing the natural world, of mentally displaying to myself a montage of images, of finally flushing out certain revelations about being. In brief, to-be-open is for me a way of philosophizing, a way of knowing that elevation of the mind so indispensable to my life.

Now, the operation to-be-open, on the day of which I am speaking, failed. From my autopsy of reality I drew only two derisory bits of information, picturesque but perfectly futile: a bird perched on the rim of a saucer was drinking the cat's milk; some other sparrows on the fence twittered as though to say such things should not be done. And that is all my philosophic observations brought me! I couldn't get over it! How could my examination have garnered so little spiritual food? Why had the world, to which I had made my act of obeisance, offered so little in return? It became clear to me, dramatically, that this paucity of meaning, all things taken into account, could be attributed only and directly to my own inner poverty.

Was I growing senile? It was certainly possible. Nevertheless, for someone retired, I still felt young. To tell the truth, a perfectly natural emotional cause might very well have been the explanation for this inertia. I had just received a call from the hospital. This call had brought me out of bed and thrown me into a state of anxiety. Six months ago my mother had been hospitalized far away in the city for an illness of old age. Every day I was afraid I might lose her. I was much attached to her: an only son, I had lived alone with her practically all my life, my father having disappeared early on.

At the beginning of her convalescence I went to visit her at the hospital every week. Gradually I began to let two weeks pass between my visits; then months. I could not bear the sad spectacle of this person, so dear to me, deformed by arthritis, helplessly suffering in her bed.

To compensate, I wrote her often. But the maternal eyes had weakened and finally she was declared blind. They had to read my letters aloud to her. Given this fact, I had decided to change my means of communication (I was never short of ideas then) and to record my missives on tape. Just the night before the fateful call, I had completed my first hour-long letter-cassette. In this way, I had told myself, she would be more independent of the nurse, and could listen to the letter as many times as she wanted.

That day, after I had looked empty-eyed at the horizon, that inadmissibly dull horizon which no longer offered a rhythm to my life, I started running along the path. I had to hurry. My mother needed me there right away, they had told me on the telephone. Her state was deteriorating quickly, I could lose her in a matter of hours. But, by chance, I had brought my letter-cassette and my tape recorder in my travelling bag. If her mind still worked, I thought, my mother would assuredly be entertained by my new idea.

The splendour of the early morning rose from the road. A sharp white light threw everything into relief. I remember. I had to slow down and finally stop. To catch my breath. To taste the morning's gifts of the instant. Suddenly reality seemed to be throwing itself at me. I was struck by an unusual apparition: a strange and solitary sunflower rose from a faraway hayfield and shone like a spotlight. Astonished, I gazed at this unexpected and unique spectacle. It would have been a worthy subject for the most beautiful photograph ever taken. I climbed a fence to approach the sunflower. The closer I got, the more I thought I could see, in its round face in the midst of its wide petals, the face of my own mother! I plunged further into the high grass, came up to the flower, inspected it with curiosity, yanked it free and took it with me. To offer to my mother. She used to love sunflowers.

I continued on my way. Cars seemed to be dragging on the

asphalt. The world moved in slow motion. Tremors ran through the muscles of my legs. I was walking so quickly that I feared I would fall and ruin my beautiful flower.

Suddenly, I remember, I must have changed direction, there were so many roads going everywhere. I had to trust them. In taking them, you think you're going to a definite place and then, without warning, just when you are confident, you find yourself somewhere else. So often roads are thought to be merely functional and insignificant. In fact, each twist and turn has its own small meaning. Twists and turns that finally unfurl into the infinity of nowhere. You think you are strong, a master of the road. Rightly or wrongly, who can say? You swallow the ribbon of pavement, you gobble down the landscape, you burn the horizon, you breathe in all the smells of the earth, you absorb the layers of air, you drink down the rain, you soak up the lakes and rivers, you chew the clouds, you devour the mountains, you tear apart the cities, the walls, the houses, take away the façades and the faces, undress the people, bring them with you. But everything both enters and leaves you, once more scatters to the wind, becomes itself the speeding whirlwind.

That too is to-be-open. To wander. To cross all things. To travel freely in the material world among the forms, without trying to seize things on the fly. To slide along the surface. To brush lightly against the real. To transform it into interior vibrations, into dreams, into memory. To dissolve into it, lose yourself, let yourself be carried away, put to sleep, raised to euphoric heights.

It was in this last stage when, exposed to the light, the full explosiveness of things and the immense universe infinitely woven around me were finally beginning to bring me to my senses, that I got to the station.

It was time. The small station was crowded with travellers. I hesitated before going inside, as though my fate was about to be decided.

As soon as I was inside, shots echoed through the building. I started violently, then stood dumbfounded. I hadn't expected such a welcome! I had the stupid reflex of trying to protect my sunflower by hiding it behind me. But it was higher than my own head.

Quickly I realized that the noise had come from a television set that a railway employee had installed on his desk. The scene reminded me of those terrible war movies which had given me so many nightmares, and which I used to watch with my mother.

I got in line to pay for my trip. I searched for the right word: a destination was necessary. I had forgotten mine. But it came back to me just in time.

There was no space to sit down in the waiting room. People travel so much. Or so many people like to wait around in stations. I felt out of place here. There were too many people for such a cramped space. You would have thought an entire village had decided to meet here. Over it all mutely hung a strange atmosphere of panic and desertion. For whatever strange reasons, all these people seemed to want to leave as quickly as possible, as though fleeing some unknown catastrophe.

For my part, calm and resigned, I cast about for a wall to lean against, but even those were occupied by standing travellers. I ended up crouched in the middle of the room. I put my bag and my sunflower on my knees, took my head in my hands, and drifted into my own thoughts.

Then the station became a huge echo chamber. Against a background of human voices, the noises of heels pounding against the tiles: of all their ways of sounding (martial clatters, pawing, sliding, buzzing ...) I was most aware of sharp clicks that reminded me both of my mother's exciting shoes when I was a child and of the cane of her later years. Of sneezes, and of coughs, and of laughs, and of cries; and of women's voices chattering; and the odours of the out-of-doors mixed with those of the café; all that mixed now with my blood, which pounded against my temples, to recreate the lost world of my family.

I would have liked to go outside for a bit to weep with nostalgia. But the floor, sweating from the heat, seemed too slippery. I was afraid I was going to pass out. Better not to move.

When I raised my eyes, I saw I was surrounded by people staring at me. Some concentrated on my face, shining with illumination, as though they feared it might endanger them. Others looked at my clothes, as though they were unsuitable. But – it has to be said – what most attracted their attention was my fabulous sunflower.

I panicked to see those millions of seconds which constitute me displayed for such shameless inspection. A billion heartbeats, small convulsions, persistent writhings, inchings forward, to arrive here, at myself, anthropoid vertebrate mammal, structure of bone and flesh, composed of water and carbon polymars, sitting stupidly on my heels, like a foetus, with my mother-sunflower, in a train station, uncomfortable under the disapproving eyes of these strangers.

I got ready to take a walk outside, whatever the cost, when a place came free on a nearby bench. I was amazed. I leapt for it with my bag and my vegetable friend. At the same time a young woman ran towards it, her arms filled with legs: she was carrying a small dog, with some half-wrapped parcels and a suitcase as well. But she arrived a second too late: I was already there. The young lady stayed standing in front of me, silent, looking me right in the eye. Perhaps she wanted to give me a lesson in politeness or humiliate me or seduce me or inspire me to have compassion for her fate. Those next to me looked me up and down disapprovingly. Why me? I asked them. I had just arrived. What about the others? All those who had had seats all along. But the poor woman is so burdened down, they were saying to me, don't you see? And I? I replied. I'm no longer twenty years old and I have my mother! This emotional argument came out unasked. Of course no one understood me. At least they didn't seem to sympathize with me. For a moment I wanted to soften and give in. But I did nothing. I crossed my hands over my sunflower, closed my eyes, and breathed easy. I should have gone to sleep to escape from all their hostility.

Suddenly the train arrived, although no one had heard it coming. Bizarre.

With surprising speed the travellers gathered together their baggage, then in a disorderly mass of colours and shapes pushed out of the room and towards the barricade.

Outside, another unpredictable element: it was starting to rain. Temperature of departures. So dark was the sky that it seemed the night had begun. But the day continued. In any case, light never dies, everyone should know that. But I thought I was seeing the sad sign of a death. I would arrive too late and would feel guilt for the rest of my life.

At the platform, we still had to wait.

For a long time.

Interminably.

The travellers, on tiptoe, craned to understand, and as no explanation appeared, they became more and more irritable. I had my own worries: my sunflower had started to wilt.

The wait ended. There was a frantic rush to climb aboard. Someone should have grabbed them by the shirt and begged them to calm down. But they were in a hurry. They were in a hurry to wait. They were in a hurry to wait inside the cars.

In the confusion of the embarkation certain vibrations in the atmosphere emanating from a throat, reached my ear: someone nearby was addressing me. It took me a long time, because you might say that I am often characterized by slowness, to realize I was being talked to. Someone wanted to exist for me. Nevertheless, the words passed in an arc above my head. It was a feminine voice. I believed I was hearing my mother. Had my giant flower begun to talk? I almost thought so, until the moment when my eyes met the body of my interlocutor. I recognized the young woman I had defied just a few moments before on the bench.

As her luminous words, filled with sweet iridescence, flowing from that unreal mouth, took on the colour of her eyes, I regretted my impoliteness. She asked me in what direction I was going. 'That way,' I replied to her, pointing west. She turned in the opposite direction. There were two trains only a few minutes apart and it was important not to confuse them. The one which had just come into the station pointed east. The young woman had made me aware of this. Overcome by melancholy and distracted as usual, I hadn't paid attention and, carried along by the human wave, was blindly following.

I thanked her sincerely and explained that it would have been a serious error for me because at this very moment my mother was dying in the hospital: I was anxious to get there, I had promised her.

All this happened as though once more I had the use of words.

'And this magnificent sunflower is for her,' I stammered out, smiling timidly. 'It's her favourite kind.'

I offered to help her: awkwardly I tried to get hold of her dog and almost dropped it.

'Take a package instead. You are very kind.'

We were pushed from behind.

'Is it a female?' I asked her naïvely, trying to tickle its muzzle with a fingertip.

'No, it's a boy,' corrected the young woman. 'Noble, that's his name. I'm taking him on holiday with me.'

'My name is Val,' I told her.

'Agatha,' she replied.

I helped her up the steps and followed her down the car to her seat. While she held my sunflower, I set her packages in the rack, started all over again, arranged them differently, as though I wanted to delay the moment of separation, started to leave, sat down beside her for a moment taking Noble in my arms so that someone could get by us. I dreamed, in a brief intoxicating flash, that I was heading east ...

The other train, the one going in the opposite direction, now made its noisy arrival. I had to change. I got up quickly and said goodbye to Agatha. She was still carrying my sunflower and held it out to give it back to me.

'This flower is even more beautiful in your hands,' I told her, flushing. 'Please be so kind as to keep it.'

And I went out, tottering.

On the platform, alone, silent and thoughtful as always, I was whistling under my breath as though to imitate, you might have said, the locomotive which was about to set off for the east.

The train was already going when, suddenly, I began to run ...

To run in an irrational way in ... the direction of ...

I leapt into Agatha's car.

Climbing up I dropped my cassette from my bag: it was immediately ground into the tracks.

GAETAN BRULOTTE was born in Lévis, Québec, in 1945. He attended the Université de Laval, then went to Paris for Graduate Studies at the Ecole des Haute Etudes en Sciences Sociales, where he worked under Roland Barthes.

On his return to Canada he began teaching French Literature at the CEGEP in Trois Rivières. He then accepted a position at the Université de Québec in Trois Rivières.

In 1979 his first novel, *L'Emprise*, was published to critical acclaim. This was followed by two books of short stories: *Le Surveillant* (1982) and *Ce qui nous tient* (1988).

Gaetan Brulotte currently teaches at the University of South Florida and is working on his second novel.

LAUSELL

Gaetan Brulotte